Nat Gould

On and Off the Turf in Australia

Nat Gould

On and Off the Turf in Australia

ISBN/EAN: 9783337314057

Printed in Europe, USA, Canada, Australia, Japan

Cover: Foto ©Andreas Hilbeck / pixelio.de

More available books at **www.hansebooks.com**

ON AND OFF THE TURF

IN

AUSTRALIA

BY

NAT GOULD

(VERAX)

AUTHOR OF "THE DOUBLE EVENT," "HARRY DALE'S JOCKEY,"
"THROWN AWAY," ETC.

LONDON

GEORGE ROUTLEDGE AND SONS, LIMITED

BROADWAY, LUDGATE HILL

MANCHESTER AND NEW YORK

CONTENTS.

ON AND OFF THE TURF.

CHAPTER I.

A PRELIMINARY CANTER.

An unpretending book. Writers on Australia. First impressions. The sort of men wanted. Prospects. Living.

BEFORE settling down into my stride, and writing an account of more than ten years On and Off the Turf in Australia, it will be better, by way of introduction, to take a preliminary canter.

This is an unpretending book, and I hope will be accepted as such by critics and readers alike. The frequent use of the personal pronoun is not egotism, but merely a matter of convenience. Many books have been written about Australia and the Australians. Some of these works show that the authors have endeavoured to find the bad, not the good, in both country and people. There is a tendency

1

to find bad instead of good in men and things, because it is easier and less trouble. Any critic will acknowledge " slating," to use a slang word, is easier than praising.

It does seem the height of presumption for men who have merely scampered through a country at the rate of a tourist, to sit down and write authoritatively about it.

Over ten years' residence in the Australian Colonies has shown me the fallacy of men attempting such works.

It must be amusing to a Colonial to read the glaring errors writers about Australia fall into, not from any desire to do so, but through ignorance.

In these pages I shall merely relate facts, and anecdotes and descriptions given are from personal knowledge of men and country. Of the Australian turf I may fairly claim to have a considerable knowledge, and it is mainly owing to the persuasion of many friends in the Colonies I am writing these reminiscences of an exceedingly pleasant sojourn there.

There is a vast difference between racing in Australia and in England, as the reader will not fail to discover if he is interested enough in the preliminary canter to go on with it to the finish.

It was shortly after Harvester and St. Gatien ran their famous dead heat for the Derby at Epsom, I sailed for Sydney. Strange to say, a horse called The Harvester won the last Derby I saw at Flemington, Melbourne, last November (1894).

It was on a sudden impulse I made up my mind to go out to Australia. What false notions I had about the Colonies were quickly discovered on arrival there. Adelaide gave the first impression of the Colonies, and it was a surprise. Big cities I had not expected to find; but here was Adelaide, not the most important, a large town.

It struck me as curious, however, in returning from the city to the pier late at night, that a gentleman, homeward bound from the theatre or an evening party, should have his upper half clothed in the regulation "waiter's outfit," while his lower extremities were encased in breeches and top-boots.

Such trifling anomalies as this are soon overcome. It is not the clothes that make the man in Australia.

A first glimpse of Melbourne shows the traveller, at a glance, that there are big cities here. It is a charming sight to enter Port Phillip Heads and sail up the fine bay. Melbourne, however, is at a great disadvantage, through being so far away from deepwater anchorage. It is the wonderful facilities of Sydney harbour for commercial purposes that must always make it *the* port of Australia.

Of Melbourne more anon. It is an extraordinary city, and during the Cup week may well be termed marvellous. Many great finishes have I witnessed for the premier race of Australia, and an account of some of them may be found interesting later on.

Sydney could not be more beautifully situated, and its harbour is one of the finest in the world. Old news this; but it will bear repeating, because it is true.

One idea I hope to be able to dispel in this preliminary canter. A man who is not much use in England will find Australia will not receive him with open arms. There is a false impression that if a man is a failure at home, he is bound to turn out a success abroad. This is wrong. Australia, if I read her people aright, does not want failures exported from England. The Colonies decline to be made a "dumping ground" for the wrecks and failures of the Mother Country.

What Australia wants, and means to get in time, is some of the backbone of Old England.

From what I have seen since my return, England has sadly neglected her farmers. It is the sons of English farmers that are wanted in the Colonies.

New South Wales' land laws have lately been altered, and liberal terms are offered to settlers.

The agricultural districts of England are the backbone—or the greater portion of it—of her prosperity, and Australia, I have not the slightest doubt, would eagerly accept this portion of the backbone.

Another word of advice, if I may give it. No man should go out to the Colonies under the impression he will not have to work. He will have to work hard; but if he be a good man, he will be well paid for what he does.

In writing of "failures," I do not allude to the man who fails to obtain work through lack of employment. Such a man might do well in Australia, because it has been no fault of his own he has not done well here.

There is plenty of wealth in the Colonies. Depression there has been, but that will soon be dispersed. A more delightful place to live in than Australia, for the general run of people, it would be difficult to find.

They know how to live and how to enjoy life there. One writer on the Colonies, who, by the bye, was a ghastly failure as a lecturer, condemns the cookery.

Australia is not a land of gourmands and gluttons, but it is a land of plenty, and, as far as cookery goes, it gives a long start to the horrible messes some people delight in.

Having taken a preliminary canter, and pulled up a trifle lame, I must get fairly going again, when I trust this lameness at the start will disappear as I warm to my work.

CHAPTER II.

TURF LIFE IN THE COLONIES.

Racing men : their superstitions.   Women backers.   Contrasts. Forestalling. Climate. Training track. Pressmen.

IN no part of the world can be found more enthusiastic followers of the turf than in Australia, and I may also add New Zealand, and that tight little island, Tasmania. Racing, in my humble opinion, is the most absorbing and interesting of sports.   To love horses is an inherent characteristic of Britishers, and the bulk of the Colonial people come from good old British stock.

In England the climate is very often dead against enjoying racing under the most favourable circumstances, but in Australia there is very little to complain of as regards the weather.

Sunny skies in that favoured island are the rule, and it is the exception and not the rule to be let in for a drenching day's sport.

Turfites all over the world are very much alike, but I doubt if there can be found as much enthusiasm in a race crowd in any part of the globe as there is in the Colonies. No matter under what circumstances racing takes place, the people enjoy it, and even the downfall of favourites has not much effect upon them. On the turf in the Colonies is an exceedingly pleasant existence. There are the usual ups and downs connected with it, and the same amount of bad luck and good luck. The same superstitions exist as in the old land, and racing men are wont to regard certain signs and omens with an amount of awe not understandable to ordinary mortals. There is the same prejudice against walking under a ladder on a race day—not for fear it might drop on the pedestrian's head, or because a brick might come down unexpectedly, but because it is unlucky.

I was seated in a tramcar one morning when a particular friend of mine stepped in and sat down. Suddenly, without a word of warning, he jumped up and rushed out again.

I looked under the seat to see if a dog had been secreted there, and had gone for his calves, but there was nothing to cause alarm in that direction.

Much to my surprise I saw him come in at the other side of the tram and quietly sit down. "What is the matter?" I asked. "Too much whiskey last night?"

"No," he replied, solemnly; "it's race day, you know, and I got in on the wrong side of the car. It's unlucky."

I suggested that getting out again and coming in at the other side did not do away with the fact that originally he had made a mistake. He acknowledged this, but added that repairing the error might lessen the unlucky consequences of his action.

Another friend, a "chief" on one of the Orient liners, whenever he went to a race meeting in Sydney invariably backed a horse whose name suggested something nautical, or reminded him of the boat he was on; and, strange to say, in several instances he won money by this plan. He backed a horse called Oroya one day, because it was named after an Orient liner, and the horse won.

Some men invariably back the first horse they see upon entering the paddock, and others back the mount of the jockey whose colours they come across first.

Later on I shall have something to say about owners, trainers, and jockeys, but in this chapter I am merely generalising.

Strange characters are to be met with on the turf in the Colonies.

Hundreds of men "live on the game," and appear to do well at it. How they live is a mystery to most people. They must have money to bet with, and to pay their expenses, and they always have a pound or two to invest upon anything they fancy.

Many of them are friends of the jockeys, and no doubt obtain information from them; and jockeys are much more ready to talk on an Australian racecourse than they are in England. These hangers-on of the turf are a nuisance to trainers, for they are constantly badgering them for tips. Women punters abound on the racecourses, and the same faces may be seen meeting after meeting. As a rule these punters are middle-aged or elderly women, although there are a few young ones to be found in this class.

It is amusing to watch the tactics of these women. Their faces show plainly the fascination gambling—not horse-racing—possesses for them. Their flushed countenances and restless expression betoken a mind and system strung to the highest pitch by the pernicious habits they have acquired, and which, alas! have thoroughly mastered them. With a purse tightly clutched in one hand, and either a satchel or an umbrella in the other, they push and jostle in the crowded ring, and dart from one bookmaker to another in their eagerness to see which horses are backed.

There is no bashfulness about these dames of the turf, and I am afraid some of them forfeit a good deal of what self-respect they may have to obtain information.

Some bookmakers, to their credit be it said, have a strong objection to bet with women; and I know more than one man in the ring who declines to wager with them. Others are not so scrupulous, and accept money, no matter from what quarter it comes.

On many occasions I have seen these women, when the race is being run, sitting on a seat in a quiet part of the course, waiting for the winner's number to be hoisted, and taking no interest in the race itself. All they think about is winning money, and for the sport itself they care very little.

There are thousands of ladies, however, at Flemington and Randwick, on Derby and Cup days, who visit the racecourse out of pure love of the sport, combined with a natural feminine desire to be seen and to see others.

The women punters, however, are a nuisance on the turf, and it is not an edifying sight to see them losing caste in the whirlpool of the betting-ring.

After considerable experience, I have found that once a woman takes to gambling, it absorbs her whole thoughts, and gambling leads to other things, such as champagne and its attendant consequences.

To the credit of the racecourse secretaries and officials, be it said, that they use every endeavour to keep loose women off their courses, and in this they succeed admirably.

It is a genuine cosmopolitan crowd on an Austra-

lian course. The Governor of the Colony appears to
forget his office for the time being, and to take a
delight in mingling with the people. A racing
Governor is bound to become popular. A Governor
who has no fondness for sports of any kind has no
hold upon the affections of the people. Lord Carrington was one of the most popular Governors New South
Wales ever had, and so was Lord Hopetoun in
Victoria, and both were real good sportsmen. In
this respect Lord Brassey should be a popular Governor, for the Australians are great yachtsmen.

Class distinctions are not so marked on Colonial
racecourses as in England. There are no reserves for
the Upper Ten, as at Ascot, Goodwood, Sandown, and
other places. The V. R. C. and the A. J. C., that is
the Victorian Racing Club and the Australian Jockey
Club, have reserves for their members, and on the
Jockey Club Stand at Randwick ladies are not
allowed, and the public can be admitted upon paying
an extra five shillings—a privilege not availed of to
any great extent. Such a reserve as that at Sandown for members of the club is unknown, and I do
not think the racing, or the pleasures connected with
it, suffer on this account. For one thing there is
far more extensive and better accommodation provided for the public in the Colonies.

Flemington and Randwick I describe later on;
but it will not be out of place to mention that the

accommodation at both these places is far ahead of
that on the principal English courses.

Racing in the Sunny South is more of a pleasure
than a business. Thousands of people are not cooped
up in small rings, as though they were so many
sheep crowded into a pen. There is plenty of elbow
room, and even on a Melbourne Cup day at Flemington there is ample room for the ladies to promenade
on the spacious lawn, although there are from fifty to
eighty thousand people present on the course. Ten
thousand is a very small attendance at a great race
meeting in Australia, although it does not reach this
number at suburban meetings, without it be an
exceptional day.

It is this feeling of freedom and comfort makes
turf life in the Colonies so enjoyable. There is so
much geniality and goodwill about it. Although
men are keen about making money, and occasionally
indulge in sharp practices, most owners are not averse
to the public knowing what their horses can do, and
what chances they have of winning. No owner I ever
met liked to be forestalled in the betting market, nor
is it natural he should be. It is not in human nature
that such should be the case. Granted the public pay
freely towards the race-fund, in the shape of gate-
money, they should not forget that keeping racehorses is a very expensive game. The public know
exactly what they pay to go to a race-meeting to

see five or six races, as the case may be—if they bet that is their look out. But an owner does not know what he is going to see. He may see something that surprises him very much, such as his horse running last when it ought to have been first, according to its trials.

Owners of racehorses have a lot to contend with, and I think they may be pardoned if occasionally they say bitter things when they find themselves forestalled in the market.

Nine months out of the twelve the climate of Australia is all that can be desired, and what more can a man expect.

The racing year commences on the 1st August, from which the ages of horses date, so that the three-year-olds running in the A. J. C. Derby the middle of September or the V. R. C. Derby in the first week in November, or the last week in October, are much younger three-year olds than those taking part in the English Derby. So favourable is the climate that flat-racing is going on all the year round, and there is no closed time, as in the old country.

Occasionally in the winter months it is necessary to wear a top-coat, but even then the sun is generally warm enough to make it pleasant. No biting east winds, or frost and snow, make racing a burden rather than a pleasure. At Christmas it is racing in sunshine to perfection, and the meeting of the A. J. C.

at Randwick on Boxing-day may be described as a few hours turned into melting moments. Many a time, as I have watched the race for the Summer Cup at Randwick, has my mind wandered to the old land, and thoughts of the snow and dull leaden sky have almost made me shiver, even with the thermometer at close upon a hundred in the shade.

Christmas in Australia is indeed a contrast to that in England. Boxing-day races in the two hemispheres are also vastly different.

In Australia we have flat-racing amidst glorious sunshine. In England races under G. N. H. Rules, probably with a white mantle of snow covering the earth. There cannot be much pleasure even in backing a winner when your fingers are almost too cold to hold the money, and it must be indeed a dreary occupation to be " out in the cold," and backing losers with the thermometer down to zero.

If Fortune be cold to us in Australia we have the consolation of knowing Nature warms towards us.

It must be very depressing to return from a racecourse with empty pockets and a thaw setting in.

Men must have strong constitutions to stand the wear and tear of English racing, season after season, and they earn the money they make.

Racing in the Colonies is conducted under most favourable atmospheric conditions as a rule, and therefore it is all the more delightful and enjoyable.

The best part of the day, in my opinion, is the early morning, and many pleasant hours have I spent on the training track watching the horses at work.

There are no restrictions placed upon the members of the sporting press watching horses do their gallops.

Formerly at Randwick anyone was allowed on the training-track, but now only those persons who have business there are permitted to be present. This is a change for the better.

Every facility is given the representatives of the various newspapers by the racecourse authorities, and with but few exceptions they are treated with courtesy and respect.

The sporting pressmen with whom I associated during my stay in the Colonies were a genial, jolly set of men, and thoroughly competent. We had some rare fun as we journeyed to the various meetings, and jokes and anecdotes flew round rapidly. Regular Bohemians they were, and warm-hearted and generous to a degree. Always ready and willing to lend a helping hand to a comrade, either in his work or when misfortune overtook him.

They were men who had many temptations thrown in their way, but kept honest and straight in their careers.

Some of the happiest days of my working life have been spent in their society, and as comrades the bulk of them were true as steel.

We had our little differences occasionally, and at times the arguments as to the merits of certain horses became heated, but all these disputes invariably ended amicably, and the discussion generally closed with, "Well, what's yours, old man?" Yes, those were jolly days, and if any of my old comrades on the Press read this book, I trust they will allow the writer to class himself as one of themselves still.

CHAPTER III.

SOME RACING STABLES AND TRAINERS.

Randwick. "Newmarket." Mr. Tom Payten. A racing centre. Mr. John Allsop. Mr. H. Raynor. Arsenal's cup. The biter bitten. Some real "fliers." Mr .James Swan. A slice of luck.

MANY of the Colonial racing stables I have seen will bear favourable comparison with those in other parts of the world. They may not be built on such an elaborate scale, but for all the purposes of training quarters they are adequate. Nothing is more delightful than to pay a visit to some well-appointed racing stable, and after inspecting the horses to have a quiet chat with the trainer in his comfortable house.

Trainers, as a rule, are reserved men, but once get them started on a favourite topic they are good company and have a large fund of anecdotes and reminiscences to draw upon.

Randwick is the headquarters of the turf in New South Wales, and I know more of it than any other racing quarter in the Colonies.

A quiet, charmingly-situated place is Randwick. Built on the rise, it commands an extensive view over the racecourse, and far away to famous Botany Bay and La Perouse. It also has an outlook over the Centennial Park, and a distant view of the city may be obtained.

Randwick is within easy distance of Sydney, about four miles or a shade more from the General Post Office, and the trams run there at frequent intervals.

Many racing men reside there, and most of them have large, comfortable residences. The king of the ring, Mr. Humphrey Oxenham, has a beautiful mansion overlooking the racecourse, fitted up in the most luxurious manner, and displaying in every room the good taste of its owner.

One of the principal racing stables is that presided over by Mr. Thomas Payten at " Newmarket," Lower Randwick. These stables were built by the Hon. James White, whose position in the Colonial racing world was similar to that held by Lord Falmouth for so many years in England.

In years gone by Mr. M. Fennelly as trainer, and Tom Hales as jockey, and the Hon. James White as owner, were quite as formidable a trio in Australia as Mr. M. Dawson, the late Fred Archer, and Lord Falmouth in England.

When Mr. Fennelly died, Tom Payten, as he is

familiarly called, took command of the Newmarket horses, and a worthy successor he proved to be.

The success of the famous "Blue and White" on the turf was wonderful; and I think, writing from memory as most of this book is written, that the stable won almost every race of importance. How many Derbies have been won by horses trained here I am afraid to say; but when I first landed in the Colonies the A. J. C. and V. R. C. Derby was regarded as a standing dish for one of Mr. White's horses. Backers looked forward with confidence to having a plunge on Mr. White's Derby colt, and, as a rule, they had occasion to rejoice after the race.

Every classic race of importance fell to the share of Mr. White's horses, and the run of successes in these races is phenomenal.

The spell was broken when Mr. White decided upon selling the greater number of his horses in training, and there is a strange similarity between the dispersal of Lord Falmouth's stud and the sale of Mr. White's horses. The majority of them turned out failures, although one or two managed to win races of a minor character. I shall have occasion to allude to some of the horses in this stable in another chapter devoted to great racers. Chester was the founder of Mr. White's stud, and he was a wonderfully good horse, and Martini-Henri also got some fair stock. Chester, however, must have been

Mr. White's favourite, and no horse better deserved that honour.

Since Mr. White's death Tom Payten has been in sole charge at Newmarket, although the ownership of the horses has changed. Mrs. White still keeps up the breeding establishment at Kirkham, and has lately imported a couple of well-bred English stallions to take the place of the defunct Chester. I think she has no reason to be dissatisfied with her success so far.

Newmarket stables are built on a large space of ground at Lower Randwick.

The trainer's residence is a fine, commodious house, and stands well back from the road in spacious grounds.

The stables are well built, and there is ample room in them. Entering a large covered building, the visitor finds himself in a spacious hall, as it were, on either side, at the far end of which are ranged large loose boxes, and above them a wide gallery goes round three sides of the building. All these boxes are kept in beautiful order, and are airy, and light, and well drained. Everything is neat and clean, as a racing stable should be, and the numerous lads are kept well in hand and are taught their business, and also, what is quite as necessary, obedience.

Tom Payten rules over all with a firm hand, and at the same time is a just master.

Many a pleasant hour have I passed in these

famous stables with the trainer, and have heard him descant with pride upon the various horses as they were led out of their boxes for my inspection. Some wonderfully good animals have tenanted these boxes. Here I have seen Abercorn, Dreadnought, Cranbrook, Carlyon, Stromboli, Trieste, Camoola, Titan, Acme, Singapore, Autonomy, Utter, Prelude, Trident, a few names dotted down at random out of a host of others of which I am reminded. Thousands of pounds have been spent upon "Newmarket," and the money has not been thrown away.

Lower down the road, on the opposite side, stands an unpretentious but cosy-looking house, and at the rear a glimpse can be caught of an extensive range of stables.

This is the abode of Mr. John Allsop, a trainer, who has rapidly come to the front during the past ten years. Mr. Allsop is a very different man from Mr. Payten, and he has very few equals as a trainer. His stables are built on three sides of a square, with a spacious yard in the centre, and every accommodation for hay and corn, and the various articles of diet race-horses require. All the loose boxes were built on the trainer's own design, and they reflect great credit upon him.

Many a good horse has John Allsop shown me in these boxes. A more devoted man to his work than Allsop I have never met. He revels in it; and

morning, noon, and night he can be found on the spot
looking after his charges. In a great measure I think
the secret of his success lies in his constant attention
to the horses under his charge. For a thing
to be well done there is nothing like doing it
yourself, and Mr. Allsop evidently knows this, and
acts accordingly.

The last time I paid him a visit, Paris, now in
England, was an inmate of his stables. He is owned
by Mrs. H. C. White, and was formerly trained by
James Monaghan, one of the good old stamp of
trainers, about whom more anon. Paris is for his
inches about one of the best gallopers I ever saw, and
he has won no end of big races. A couple of Caulfield
Cups falling to his share.

Cremorne, Trenchant, Tiwona, Sundial, Atlas,
and others were in the comfortable boxes. One of
the best horses Allsop has had in my time was
Gibraltar, and it was most unfortunate when he
broke down in Melbourne. In the dining-room at
Mr. Allsop's are portraits in oils of most of the good
horses he has trained, and he is not a believer in the
superstition that after a horse's picture has been
painted he never wins a race.

This chapter is merely a cursory one about trainers,
and I shall have more to say about them in anecdotal
form when dealing with the horses under their charge.
No excuse, however, need be offered for noticing them

here, as every man mentioned more than deserves all that I write about him.

Leaving Mr. Allsop's and crossing the road, we come to the stables occupied by Mr. H. Raynor, a trainer, like Mr. Monaghan, of the old school. Harry Raynor's face is familiar at all the principal race meetings. He has not what may be called a charming countenance, nor is he much of a lady-killer, but he knows his business thoroughly. He generally appears in the paddock on race days in a slouch hat, and almost invariably carries an umbrella. He looks more like an old bush hand than one of the cutest trainers at Randwick.

Many a good thing has Harry Raynor been in during his time. He trained for the late Mr. W. Gannon up to the time of his death. At one time Mr. Gannon acted as starter to the A. J. C., and he was well known as the host of Petty's Hotel in Sydney. A stout, florid-looking man, with a good deal of the cut of an old English farmer about him. Some curious yarns are told about Mr. Gannon and his trainer, and one in particular tickled me immensely. It shows how the biter was bitten in this case with a vengeance.

Strange to say the story was related to me by a well-known squatter and horse-breeder, as we returned from a trip to Hobart in the SS. "Oonah," with that prince of skippers, Captain Featherstone, in command.

Mr. W. Gannon owned a horse called Arsenal, a good animal, and Harry Raynor trained it. The horse was much fancied by his owner for the Melbourne Cup, and Mr. Gannon determined to be in the market in time and get the cream of the betting. He accordingly instructed a well-known commissioner at that time to take the long odds to a considerable amount for him. Instead of doing what he ought in fairness to have done, the commissioner let another big backer and horse-owner into the secret. The odds were duly accepted, but the long prices were returned to, I will call him Mr. B., and the shorter odds to the owner, Mr. Gannon. Naturally Mr. Gannon was riled at not obtaining a longer price, and he determined to get even with Mr. B.

Shortly before the Cup was due to be run, Mr. Gannon was staying at Menzies Hotel, in Melbourne, Mr. B. was also there, and the pair were good friends. One evening, at dinner, Mr. Gannon received a telegram. He opened it leisurely, not deeming it of much importance, and read it.

Its contents apparently had an effect on him, for he gave vent to some expressions more powerful than polite.

"What's the matter?" asked Mr. B., who was sitting opposite to him. "Anything wrong with the horse?"

Mr. Gannon handed the telegram across the table,

and when Mr. B. glanced at it he, too, became very serious.

The telegram was from Harry Raynor, to the effect that Arsenal had gone wrong, and it was doubtful if he could start for the Cup.

Mr. B. thanked Mr. Gannon for showing him the telegram, and he intimated his intention of getting rid of the bulk of the money he had taken about the horse by laying it off.

This laying-off business was put into the hands of a commissioner, who commenced operations at once. As fast as the money was laid off, another well-known backer was taking up the wagers in favour of Arsenal.

Mr. B. knew this gentleman, and thinking to warn him against backing a " dead un," said, " It is no business of mine, but are you backing Arsenal for yourself? If so, let some one else have a bit of it. It's my money that is being laid off; the horse has gone wrong."

" That's strange," said the backer, who knew nothing of the telegram business.

" Why ? " asked Mr. B. " What is strange ? "

" Well, I'm backing it for the owner," was to Mr. B. the astounding answer.

Mr. B. commenced to smell mischief. He went to his commissioner and asked him not to lay any more Arsenal money off.

" I can't," was the laconic reply; " I've laid it all off already."

" And Gannon's got it," was Mr. B.'s comment.

It was quite true. Mr. Gannon had paid the backer in his own coin, and no doubt he chuckled to himself on the success of the telegram.

As a matter of fact, Arsenal did go off his feed before the Melbourne Cup he won, and his clever trainer had an unthankful task in getting him to the post all right.

Another good horse I saw in Harry Raynor's stable was the Australian Peer. I first saw this colt in Brisbane on the Eagle Farm racecourse. I knew his owner, Mr. W. H. Kent, well, and he bought the Peer's dam, Stockdove, with the foal at foot.

The Australian Peer was sold to Mr. Gannon for, I think, seven hundred guineas, and a contingency if he won the Derby, which he afterwards did. I sent the telegram from the Brisbane office, on behalf of the owner, that clinched the bargain. Needless to say, I watched the career of the Peer with interest. He was a good colt, but a terrible high galloper, and his front action was, I think, detrimental to him. He used to gallop with his knees almost up to his nose. He created a great surprise when he beat Trident in a three-mile race at Randwick.

Another great galloper in Raynor's stable at the time of my last visit was Bungebah. He is a chestnut gelding, and a veritable flier. It was at one time a moot point as to whether Bungebah, Marvel, Paris, or Carbine were not about equal over a mile w. f. a.* Melos, in this stable, was a good horse, but he was unlucky to bump up against such a pair as Abercorn and Carbine in nearly every w. f. a. race. He had the honour of beating Carbine in the V. R. C. Champion Stakes, at level weights, the three miles being run in 5.51.

Gatling, purchased by Mr. Gannon from Mr. Dan O'Brien for, I think, two thousand guineas, was a failure. He was a handsome horse, but developed temper, although Mr. O'Brien has assured me he was perfectly quiet when he had him. It was a pity Mr. Gannon did not secure Carbine instead of Gatling ; but that is all in the luck of racing.

James Swan has an establishment not far from Raynor's, and although he has not had the best of luck in late years, it may change for the better. I once bought a mare off Swan, named Optima, for a gentleman in Brisbane, and she ran well in the Queensland capital.

I shall not forget the day I bought her, in a hurry. It turned out a very wet one, in more senses than one. It was at Canterbury Park, a suburban course near Sydney. I had dined with a few friends, and I well remember we all backed Optima after the purchase,

* Weight for age, whenever used in the book.

and she lost.   I also recollect the mare nearly did for
me as she went out of the paddock, for she lashed out
and just missed my lower extremities.   It was a
narrow squeak ; I do not want another such.   Swan
had a slice of luck when Regina won the last V. R. C.
Oaks for that good sportsman, Mr. J. J. McManus ;
but had Quiver got off, she would probably have
landed the race.

Quiver had C. Moore on her, and was a hot
favourite.   When Mr. Watson started the mares,
Quiver did not go.   Moore, instead of sailing after
the others, quietly walked Quiver back into the
enclosure.   There was a scene, of course.   An inquiry
was held by the stewards.   Result : Moore was sus-
pended, and he soon afterwards left for San Fran-
cisco.   I saw Moore in Sydney before he sailed, and
he assured me that he lost his head entirely when
Quiver was left at the post, but that he had no
intention of doing anything crooked.   At any rate,
Moore's action was the cause of James Swan having a
slice of luck with Regina.

CHAPTER IV.

MORE ABOUT STABLES AND TRAINERS.

Mr. Hordern's racers. Nordenfeldt. Dan O'Brien. Some
experiences. The egg-boiler. Two fortunes missed. Harry
Giltinan. Mark Thompson. Mr. Noud's hospitality. The
result. A couple of aldermen. Mr. W. Kelso.

TURNING up the road towards Sydney again, the
stables of Mr. Sam Hordern are soon reached. Mr.
Hordern is the head of the house of Anthony Hordern
and Sons, the "Whiteley's" of Australia. He has
an immense business and is a very rich man. Mr.
Hordern has not long been a patron of the turf, but
once he launched upon a racing career he spent money
with a lavish hand, and bought the highest-priced
and best-bred youngsters he could purchase.

In addition to his racing stables he has a large
stud farm, and the lord of the harem there is Nordenfeldt, by Musket—Onyx. This horse was sold by the
late Mr. James White to the Sylvia Park Stud, New
Zealand, from whom he bought him for 1200 guineas
as a yearling, and was purchased by Mr. Hordern for

5600 guineas, this being, at the time, the highest price
ever given for a thoroughbred in Australia. It has
since been largely exceeded by the sale of Carbine to
the Duke of Portland, for 13,000 guineas. Nordenfeldt
was a cheap horse. He has sired some wonderfully good
stock—perhaps Strathmore being the best of his get,
although Zalinski and Carnage were great horses.
All three were owned by Mr. W. R. Wilson, of the
St. Albans Stud, Victoria. Nordenfeldt's dam, Onyx,
is by Angler, out of Chrysolite, by Stockwell, and
Angler, as his name indicates, is by Fisherman.
Fisherman was imported by the Messrs. Fisher from
England. The late Sir John Astley, in his wonderfully interesting book, has a lot to say about old
Fisherman ; and he considers it was a disgrace to let
him leave England. In Fisherman, as in the case of
Musket, what proved to be England's loss turned out
Australia's gain. Since writing the above I learn
Nordenfeldt is dead, and Mr. Hordern will replace
him with a St. Simon horse. Mr. Hordern's stud
farm is at Picton, within easy distance of Sydney ;
and he has there a fine lot of mares, some of which
were bought for him by Mr. F. W. Day, his former
trainer, who was sent over to select them. Thousands of pounds have been spent by Mr. Hordern
during the last few years upon blood stock ; but so
far he has not met with much success on the turf,
although he won the Sydney Cup with Realm, a horse

he bought from the late Capt. Sandeman, who died in England a short time back.

Mr. Hordern's stables at Randwick are quite new, and cost a lot of money, and they are perhaps the best of their kind in the Colonies.

When he started racing he selected Mr. F. W. Day—who had been in practice as a veterinary surgeon at Randwick—as his trainer. Mr. Day is now at Cheltenham, where he is following his profession. When Mr. Day relinquished his charge of the horses, Mr. Ike Earnshaw accepted Mr. Hordern's offer to train for him, and left his old quarters at Moorefield—where he had been a public trainer—to take up his residence at Randwick. Ike Earnshaw is well known and respected in the racing world in the Colonies, and although he has not prepared many winners for Mr. Hordern at present, with the class of horses he has to work upon, it should not be long before he saddles up some winners of big races. When he is desirous of possessing a horse, Mr. Hordern does not stick at the price, and such a man deserves to succeed. In addition to racing Mr. Hordern is a good all-round patron of sport, as the cricketers, yachting men, and footballers have reason to know.

Next door to Mr. Hordern's modern stables is Mount Vernon, the residence of Mr. Dan O'Brien, one of the best known racing men in Australasia.

It was Mr. O'Brien who purchased Carbine as a

yearling, and sold him to Mr. Donald Wallace for 3000 guineas.

It is not many months since I looked over the new stables Mr. O'Brien has built at Mount Vernon.

He has shown excellent judgment in designing them, and although he has not accommodation for more than a dozen horses there is ample space to enlarge them.

One of the finest views in Sydney can be obtained from the look-out tower at the top of these stables. With the aid of a powerful glass the trial gallops on Randwick racecourse can be seen, and I have no doubt Mr. O'Brien has seen many a good go from his race observatory. The view extends over the Centennial Park, and the various public buildings in the city can be easily picked out.

Mr. O'Brien commenced his turf career in New Zealand when very young, and, step by step, he has risen until he has become one of the most famous trainer-owners. Many good horses he has owned, amongst the best being Trenton, by Musket, now doing stud duty at Mr. Wilson's at St. Alban's, and Carbine. When I last looked round the stables he had a good horse in Loyalty—since gone to the stud—and Launceston Response and Bob Ray, a real good youngster, were also there. Loyalty, as a three-year old, won several w. f. a. races, and gave promise of having a brilliant career, and he also ran a great

race in the Melbourne Cup, finishing fourth to Tarcoola, Carnage, and Jeweller; he also landed the
Melbourne Stakes, after a desperate finish with Newman. It was reported that Mr. O'Brien had an offer
of 2000 guineas made for the colt, but he informed me
such was not the case. I fancy that price would have
tempted him to part with the son of St. George.

Mr. O'Brien's experiences have been varied, and
when chatting in his snuggery, surrounded by pic-
tures of famous horses he has owned and cups
and trophies he has won, the time passes quickly
enough. In the days when Mr. O'Brien was riding
in New Zealand, racing was far different to what it is
now. He had his ups and downs, and was glad
enough at times to land a hack race.

On one occasion there were three starters in a hack
race in which he rode. The favourite was, of course,
considered a real good thing, but the best laid
schemes occasionally go wrong.

When the jockey on the favourite saw one of the
other horses was going to beat him, he coolly leaned
over and pulled his opponent out of the saddle.

"Even then he didn't win," said Dan O'Brien,
with a chuckle, "as I came up on the other side and
beat him."

Trainers are great believers in the time test when
trying horses in the Colonies, and all sorts of devices
are resorted to in order to put the clockists out.

Watches are all very well, but I think not many trials have been timed with an egg-boiler, yet such was the case on one gallop.

It appears that from a house overlooking the race-course Mr. O'Brien saw a couple of horses just about to break off for a " go."

Not having his watch handy, he seized an egg-boiler, and as the horses started set it going. He laid it flat as they passed the post.

Then he got his watch, turned up the egg-boiler again, and timed the sand as it ran out. Result : he got the correct time almost to a tick, but I never heard whether it did him much good. At all events, it was ingenious, and shows Mr. O'Brien is not short of resource. As a judge of horses, especially young stock, Mr. O'Brien has not many equals, and he has made some clever and profitable deals in his time. His judgment is seldom at fault, and he has been the founder of his own fortunes.

Two fortunes he narrowly missed landing. One when Trenton just missed the Melbourne Cup, and the other when he sold Carbine, although at the time that was a good deal. He has, however, landed some big wagers, and I trust it will be a long time before he will be short of a " merry monk," as the useful sum of £500 is generally called.

Mr. James Monaghan is another Randwick trainer, whose stables I have visited. I saw the great

Marvel there, and also Paris before he went into
Allsop's quarters.   Scores of good horses have passed
through " Jimmy's " hands, and he is one of the few
trainers of the old school left.

I am afraid space will not permit me to do more
than briefly allude to the bulk of the trainers, but if I
omit any they may rest assured it is not my fault, for
I have invariably been treated with the greatest
courtesy by them.

Among other well-known men I have met is young
Harry Giltinan, a trainer who is rapidly coming to the
front, and who has won a lot of races with not over
brilliant horses : all the more credit to him.   Chatham
was a good horse, and he won several races with him,
and Pharamond was another fair animal, although not a
beauty to look at.   Cumberoona, in his stable, was
about the best hurdle horse in Sydney when I left.

Mr. Mark Thompson trains for Mr. H. Oxenham,
and there are few abler men than he.   Mark is not a
man to waste his words.   That silence is golden he
firmly believes, and it takes a waggon and horses to
draw him out.   To look into Mark's face is to realize
the fact that there is occasionally an affinity between a
trainer and a parson.   Mark Thompson would make
up as an excellent representative of the black cloth
brigade.   Solanum, Utter, and Pilot Boy were three
good horses he made the most out of.   Utter is a mare,
but no matter.   Mares are horses but horses are not

mares. Cerise and Blue was about the best mare
Mr. Oxenham ever owned, and she did much to lay
the foundation of his fortune.

Mr. W. Duggan is another trainer I have had many
a pleasant chat with, and there are few men who have
not a good word for Mr. W. Noud. Mr. Noud is
getting on in years, but he is hale and hearty. He
handled Marvel at one time to his sorrow, but I hardly
think he was to blame in the matter. I recollect one
night I remained rather late at Mr. Noud's hospitable
house. My pony was a frisky animal, and on the way
home he took it into his head to career along Randwick
Road at a pace not ordinarily seen there. Probably
Mr. Noud's special mixture had made me as lively as
the pony, for I let him have his head. About half-
way down Randwick Road I passed Rowley Pickering,
"Nemo," of the *Sydney Mail,* and a brother pressman, in his trap with his wife, and he gave chase.

He exhorted me in a loud voice to desist from
furious driving, but as he was coming after me at the
same pace, I failed to see the joke.

Eventually, however, I pulled up, and "Nemo"
would insist upon taking the reins and driving me
home. I merely mention this incident to throw a light
upon the strength of Mr. Noud's "hospitality."

Mr. Tom Lamond is another trainer of note, whose
Zetland Lodge stables are generally filled with good
horses. The "Alderman," such he is, I believe, for the

borough of Waterloo, is a first-class trainer. It is put on
record that when asked what his special qualifications
for holding the high office of Mayor of Waterloo were,
he stated that he had won the Maribrynong Plate so
many times, and that ought to be enough to satisfy any
man. Certainly Mr. Lamond won the chief two-year-old
race of the year several times with horses trained by
him, but it is probable the members of the Social
Purity Society would not consider this a qualification
for the office of Mayor.

Zetland Lodge is a comfortable, old-fashioned
residence surrounded by a paddock in which a number
of thoroughbreds can generally be seen taking afternoon exercise. The stables, too, are old and overgrown
with ivy, and there is a bell-tower and a clock, which
give the yard quite an English appearance. Mr. Lamond
trains for Mr. Walter Hall, an immensely rich man,
and one of the noted Mount Morgan gold mine Halls.
Oxide and Delaware were a couple of the best horses
Mr. Hall had there, but the list of victories Mr. Lamond
has won would fill several pages.

. I must not omit Mr. Sam Fielder, who trains his
own horses, and also his sons. All the young Fielders
can ride, and his eldest son—Jack Fielder—is one of
the best jockeys in Australia. Three brothers, all good
jockeys, are not often met with in a family. Sam Fielder
generally confesses, when put to it, that " Jack " is
the most profitable horse he ever had in his stable.

Mr. William Kelso, of Orville Lodge, generally has from twenty to thirty horses in his stables. Mr. Kelso is a dapper man, a perfect lady-killer in his younger days. He is a man warranted not to age, and he can beat many a young hand now. He has the reputation of winning more races in the course of a season than any other trainer; and although he does not fly at high game often he makes a very good thing out of the numerous minor events he wins. He won the last Maribrynong Plate for Mr. Justin McSweeney, with Arihi, a remarkably smart filly, and at one time I saw that flying mare Mitrailleuse in his stables. Victor Hugo was a horse he won no end of races with under big weights. Mr. Kelso is excellent company, and always ready for a practical joke or an unlimited supply of good-natured chaff. His son, W. Kelso, jun., is about the best horseman at Welter weights in the Colonies.

Mr. E. Keys is another trainer who ran for the Aldermanic Stakes and won, and, I believe, since he occupied a seat on the Waverley Council it is wonderful how the roads have improved in his locality. Mr. Keys holds the record for " taking the kettle " when there is any yarn-spinning going on, but he is a good trainer and a " jolly little chap all round." He had a rattling good horse in Sir William, who ran second in the Melbourne Cup to Malvolio, and did " Teddy " out of a big win. Mr. Keys, however, generally comes up

smiling, and it is a very hard knock that makes him
flinch.   Mahee was another good horse he had.

Of Mr. W. Forrester and the Warwick Farm stables
more anon.   Other good trainers I know are Messrs.
Joe Cook, Harry Walsh of Queensland, and Watty
Blacklock from the same place, Joe Burton of
Bathurst, Dick O'Connor, and several more.

On the Victorian side Mr. Walter Hickenbotham
and Mr. James Redfearn are the two I know best, and
better men I never want to meet.   Both these gentlemen I have alluded to elsewhere.

I trust these two chapters will not prove tedious
reading, but I felt that in a book of this description
I ought to mention the names of the men who undertake the arduous and difficult duties of training
racehorses.

There are, of course, many more excellent trainers
in the Colonies, but I shall only write about men and
matters I know.   I trust before I have finished the
reader will have been interested and amused, and also
have learned something of turf life in the Colonies.
Mr. Kelly Maitland's name I omitted.   I have known him
for some years.   He is a man well known in India and
China, and also the Colonies.   When in Sydney he
managed Captain Sandeman's horses, and he owned
Greygown when Highborn just beat him in the Sydney
Cup.   Mr. Maitland always declares Greygown won
this race.   Mr. Maitland is a constant frequenter of

the training tract at Caulfield, and he is generally well up in the work the horses trained there have done. I remember he informed me of the wonderful improvement Titan had made before he beat Bel Giorno in the Toorak Handicap. Mr. Maitland is generally credited with knowing his way about. I can bear out all Captain Hayes writes about him in his interesting book, " Among Men and Horses," as Mr. Maitland has often related his experiences in India and China to me.

CHAPTER V.

Betting. A word of advice. The clubs. Sweeps. Double.
event shops. Odds laid. Back a double. The roof falls
in. The ring growing. Mr. H. Oxenham. Some big
wagers. Enormous business. Thousands at stake.
Charlie Samuels. A crack-runner. Commissioners.

THE members of the ring in Australia are a respect-
able body of men, although an undesirable person is
occasionally to be met with. Betting is inseparable
from horse-racing, and there are some heavy plungers
on the Colonial turf. I am not a heavy bettor myself,
and am none the worse off for it, although I must
confess I cannot help having an occasional flutter
when I fancy there is anything good on. If a young
man, anxious to gamble on horse-racing, asked me the
best system to adopt, I should strongly advise him to
systematically keep his money in his pocket, and not
bet at all. Few frequenters of the turf, however,
can desist putting a pound or two on when they have
a fancy. It is a bad practice for any man to bet if the

excitement of gambling obtains such a hold upon him that he cannot resist it. Never book a wager, but always bet ready money, and then you will be certain of having no black Mondays for settling on. Also never bet more than you can well afford to lose, and then not much harm will come of it.

The two principal clubs in Australia, I mean sporting clubs, are Tattersalls' in Sydney and the Victorian Club in Melbourne. There are also clubs in Adelaide and Brisbane.

Sydney Tattersalls' is one of the best appointed clubs of its kind in the world. The building cost a lot of money, and the main room, where the business is transacted, is a model of luxury. Mr. Perry is the secretary, and an admirable man for the position. The Victorian Club in Melbourne is not so elaborate as that in Sydney, but it is adequate for all requirements, and during Cup week it is a busy place. Mr. Haydon is the secretary, and has managed it for many years.

It is surprising, considering the population, what an enormous amount of money is turned over on the Colonial turf in a year. Hundreds of thousands of pounds change hands in betting with the bookmakers, and by means of the Totalisator in Queensland and South Australia. In addition to this, many thousands of pounds pass through the hands of sweep promoters, and, a year or two back, I should say half a million of

money was invested in sweeps on the Melbourne Cup
alone. This sounds big, but it is under rather than
over the mark.

In Sydney there are scores of shops where double
event betting takes place on all local events of any
importance, and on every horse and pony meeting
held during the week.

Lists are openly posted up in these shops, which
are supposed merely to be kept for the sale of
tobacco, etc. A few cigars may be seen in the
window, but the proprietor would probably be
astounded if anyone asked for them. Of course all
this is illegal; but the police take the whole thing as a
matter of course, and the law is openly set at defiance.
A raid is made upon these shops at intervals, and the
proprietors are summoned, and fined a small amount,
which they willingly contribute to the revenue of a
grateful country. Three or four years ago matters in
this direction were much worse than when I left in
the present year. A sentence of a month or three
months' imprisonment, without the option of a fine,
has had a salutary effect. The "double event" men
had no objection to paying a fine; but when it came
to a question of three months' hard, it was a very
different matter.

The odds in these shops were laid to a shilling, and it
was in former days no uncommon thing to see as much
as fifty to a hundred pounds to a shilling, and more, laid

on a Caulfield and Melbourne Cup. Twenty pounds to a
shilling, and sometimes more, could be obtained about
a double at a Saturday suburban meeting. Thousands
of pounds passed through the hands of these double
event layers, and some of the big men in the ring at
last found it necessary to start "Silver-books," as they
are termed, to oblige their humbler customers. I well
recollect backing a winning double with Joe Phillips,
of Market Street. "Joseph" kept the usual tobacconist's shop, and at the rear of it you could loll back in
a chair and allow the barber to operate on your chin.
Shaving has a soothing effect if the razor is not like a
hand-saw, and puts one into a contemplative frame of
mind. It must have been the extra good shave that
gave me luck; for as I went out of the room into the
shop, I asked "Joe" what he would lay Wild Rose
and Highborn for the Newmarket Handicap and Australian Cup. "Four hundred to one are the odds,"
he responded, and I put down my coin, and he booked
the bet.

It came off, and the very next morning the ceiling
of Joseph's shop fell in. When I got into town and
went to collect my money, I found the merry bookie
up to his knees in debris.

"No wonder the roof fell in," said Joe, when he
saw me smiling in the doorway. "Fancy you backing
a winning double."

Joe Phillips always swears it was this remarkable

circumstance that made his ceiling give way. Anyhow, I got my money, and we knocked down a bottle at " Sam's," next door.

Such wagers as these do no man any harm.

But to the ring and the men in it. First and foremost, the leader of the ring is Mr. Humphrey Oxenham, a man who has the goodwill of all classes. To show the respect in which he is held, I have only to say that before he left on a trip to the old country, a banquet was tendered him in the Town Hall, at which the Minister of Justice presided, and the then Premier, Sir George Dibbs, sent a neatly-worded apology for his absence. "All sorts and conditions of men" were present, and amongst them Members of Parliament *ad lib.* It was a glorious success, and we had a fine time of it.

Mr. Oxenham's transactions in the ring are all on a large scale, and in giving a description of his mode of carrying on business, a very fair idea will be obtained of the Australian ring generally.

The " Leviathan," as he is generally called, is a personal friend of mine, and I have always found him a genuine, upright man, a good husband and father, a generous, high-minded citizen. Mr. Oxenham is liberal, very liberal, and his hand is always in his pocket when help is needed. How much he gives away in the course of a year I cannot say, but it must be a very large sum. No deserving case is ever passed unnoticed by him, and many a man hard up has had cause to bless him.

Mr. Oxenham has places of business in Sydney, Melbourne, and Brisbane; and in addition to his large bookmaking transaction he now runs " sweeps." His name is known throughout Australasia, and a cheque signed Humphrey Oxenham would be accepted as readily as coin of the realm. Mr. Oxenham's ramifications extend from Thursday Island on the one hand to West Australia on the other, and all the intervening territory is represented on his books. Even from India, Fiji, and New Caledonia, money is sent for him to invest.

I have had opportunities of glancing over Mr. Oxenham's books, and have noted " books " to the amount of £100,000 on a single big race meeting. Last year (1894) was a quiet year on account of the depression, but on the Caulfield and Melbourne Cup Meetings he had books to the extent of £63,000 open. He laid £10,000 on the Caulfield Cup; £15,000 the Melbourne Cup; £5,000 the Derby; £10,000 the Two Cups double; £10,000 the Derby and Cup double; £10,000 the treble—two Cups and Derby; £2,000 at starting price; and £1,000 places: in all, £63,000.

The year Malvolio won the Melbourne Cup (1891), Mr. Oxenham lost £30,000 over the winner, and yet he had such an enormous amount of money in his book that he actually came out a winner on the race.

Had an outsider won what a haul he wou'd have had.
Very liberal odds are laid by the ring over such races
as the Caulfield and Melbourne Cups. A month before the Caulfield Cup race last year (1894), when
Paris won, nearly seventy horses were quoted in Mr.
Oxenham's list at 50 to 1, and more than that number in the Melbourne Cup. When Glenloth won the
Melbourne Cup in 1892, a 100 to 2 could have been
had on the course. When Tarcoola won the following year I saw 40 to 1 laid against him; and when
Patron won last November 33 to 1 could be had.
When Carbine won it was a difficult matter to get
money on at all, even at 4 or 5 to 1 in the ring;
and I believe on the day of the race, in Sydney, some
infatuated backers accepted 2 to 1 about his chance.

In 1893 Mr. Oxenham had very large volumes on
races. I saw in his book as much as £15,000 laid in
a single wager over the Derby and Cup, and there
were plenty of £10,000 and £5,000 wagers. That
year he laid what to most men would have been a
fortune against Carnage, and the colt ran second. In
the Caulfield Cup that year I saw he had laid in one
hand £5,000 to £200 Cremorne; Fulham £10,000 to
£400. Against Brockleigh £4,000, £3,000, and £2,000
wagers followed in succession. There were wagers
invested from the modest sov. to the " merry monkey "
(£500).

Betting on a Melbourne Cup commences six

months before the race, and an occasional wager is recorded before that. In addition to Mr. Oxenham, there are many bookmakers with big volumes on this great race. Mr. Jack Cohen, of Melbourne, lays in thousands; also Mr. Alf. Josephs, the leader of the Victorian ring. Mr. Sam Allen is a good bettor. Mr. Charles Westbrook makes a big book, and Paddy Burke is as genial a man as there is in the ring. I ought to have mentioned that in 1893 Mr. Oxenham laid £32,000 against Cremorne for the Melbourne Cup, and, if I recollect rightly, the horse ran about last. He laid £30,000 against Camoola, and the same amount against Jeweller, who finished third.

It takes a large staff of clerks to look after such a business as Mr. Oxenham's, and it is a very poor day's work in the Sydney establishment when a couple of hundred pounds is not taken. Mr. Tom Rose manages this department, and a right good fellow he is. He is rightly named, for he generally looks on the rosy side of life. Many a yarn have I had with him over a choice cigar and a drop of the "cratur." Tom Rose knows a heap about footracing, and he had a lot to do with that champion aboriginal runner, Charlie Samuels, who downed Hutchins. He spins yarns by the hour about the prowess of Samuels. On one occasion Tom Rose took Samuels over to North Shore to run a trial. This was soon after the blackie came down from Queensland, and

4

very little was known about him. A crack runner was put up against him, and gave Charlie a start. The black fellow won easily. Rose then suggested Samuels should give the other man a start, which he did, and again romped in, much to the surprise of the said flier. Samuels was a wonderful runner, and won no end of handicaps and matches. On one occasion, when he had won several thousands for Mr. Lees and others he was asked how much money he wanted. The darkie said he had no use for money, but would like a *saddle*. I believe a saddle was bought for him, but I never heard whether he ever used it. The last I heard of this champion runner was that he was living with a lot of blacks at a dirty poverty-stricken camp they had pitched at Botany, or in that direction. Rum, I expect, proved stronger than his resolution.

There are very few commissioners in the Colonies, the bulk of the big orders being confined to four or five men. Most owners either bet themselves or get friends to put money on for them. Mr. Phil Glenister is the best known and most popular commissioner, and scores of big transactions have been entrusted to him. Mr. Glenister is a good all-round sportsman, and is a don hand at the trap, as the blue rocks know to their cost. He has done some good shooting at pigeons in his time. He is also a very fair billiard player. Mr. Glenister is a quiet, modest man, and invariably treats people with respect. Mr. Sam

Bradbury also has a large number of commissions entrusted to him, and he bets freely when he has a good thing on.

Taken all round the ring-men are a solid lot of men, and to be a member of Tattersalls' or the Victorian Club is a guarantee of financial stability.

The billiard tournaments at both these clubs are well worth seeing, and there is a lot of betting over the result. Handsome prizes are given, and the winner is generally a good all-round player.

CHAPTER VI

How Totalisators are worked. Arguments for and against. Big dividends. Struggling crowds. Owners' tactics. Tote shops. How they were run. Double event dodges. Sweeps. "Tattersalls" and "Oxenhams." Some lucky winners. Owners' demands. A moral Government.

In Queensland, South Australia, New Zealand, and Tasmania, the totalisator on racecourses is legalised, so much per cent. on the investments being paid to the Treasury.

Opinions are fairly divided as to whether the totalisator system, or betting with bookmakers, is the more equitable and satisfactory plan of making wagers.

I saw a good deal of the working of the totalisator in Queensland, more especially at the headquarters of the Queensland Turf Club at Eagle Farm.

Undoubtedly the totalisator has many advantages over the system of betting with bookmakers for men who do not make large wagers. For the public who invest sums ranging from ten shillings upwards to, say, five pounds, the totalisator is a very handy medium. For owners who bet heavily I think the old plan of wagering with bookmakers is the best.

Ten years ago the totalisator was worked in a very primitive manner; but when Mr. Harris put up his patent at Eagle Farm there was a decided change for the better. Instead of the old blocks from which tickets had to be torn, much in the manner as dates are torn off an almanack block, a brand new machine was erected. This machine, or rather machines, were in a long wooden building, erected between the paddock and the outside, and a dividing fence between. In the paddock pound tickets were taken. On the outside 10s. tickets could be obtained. A staff of men were inside the building issuing tickets. A number board was placed outside the machine. It was a square front, and on it the names of the starters were placed, with their numbers on the card. At the head of the board was a place for showing the total amount of money put on all the horses in the race. This total, divided by the number on any particular horse, gave the exact dividend that would be returned if the horse won.

In this manner an investor could tell what horse was favourite, and also the horse that would pay the largest dividend. I have known men take a ticket on each starter in a race, and come out a winner.

When a ticket is taken on a certain horse, a bell

rings, and the number is added to the investments already made, and the total amount is increased at the top. For instance, there is a horse called Pirate, No. 10. An investor puts five pounds on No. 10. He receive five tickets, or one five pound ticket, and the bell rings five times, registering a pound wager on No. 10 each time. The total at the top, which stood at 200 before the five pounds were invested, now totals 205.

If an owner puts fifty pounds on his horse on the totalisator at one time, it naturally attracts the attention of the public, who are watching the board, and they follow his lead. Every pound invested by outsiders lessens the owner's dividend. He does not get a certain amount of odds to his fifty pounds, but has to take his share of the dividend with the general public.

This is where the shoe pinches with most owners when the totalisator is mentioned. An argument one well-known owner used against the machine, when I asked his opinion, was as follows :

" Suppose I have a horse in a race, and I put a score on him. Then suppose half-a-dozen people I know ask me if I fancy my horse's chance. If I say 'Yes,' they at once go and back it on the machine, and every pound they put on lessens my dividend. If, therefore, I want fair odds against my horse, I have to keep my information to myself.

"Take the other side of the question. If I take £200 to £20 about my horse from a bookmaker, I know exactly the amount I have to draw if it wins. I can tell my friends I fancy my horse, because, no matter how much they put on him, I have my £200 to £20 to draw if he wins."

This is, I think, a reasonable way of regarding the matter.

The totalisator is a great help to a struggling race club. In Brisbane ten per cent. was deducted from the amount invested, and if £10,000 went through the machine, as it often did, the club drew a thousand of it. I hardly think they receive so much now, as the Government claims a share of it. If totalisators were used at Flemington and Randwick, the V. R. C. and the A. J. C. would take many thousands of pounds in percentages. This money, if added to the stakes to be run for, might induce the majority of owners to regard the machine with more favour.

Personally, I prefer the old-fashioned system to the totalisator. I do not think, excepting in rare cases of rank outsiders winning, the totalisator returns better odds than the bookmakers. In the case of favourites I am sure it does not.

Some big dividends, as much as £200 for a pound are declared; but these are the exception and not the rule. I do not pretend to say that in the case of a £200 to one dividend a bookmaker would have laid these odds; but I am certain the price against the favourite in the same race, on the machine, would be no better, if as good, as that laid by the book-makers.

Then, again, it is a desperate struggle at times to obtain tickets on the totalisator, especially if it has been left until the horses are at the post. As soon as they are off, the machine is shut down, and there is no chance of making a bit in running.

I have seen a crowd of men and women struggling to get at the ticket-window, in much the same manner they fight to gain admission to a London pantomime on Boxing-night. The struggle is des-perate at times. I once saw a lady lose a portion of her attire in the fray, that necessitated her speedy withdrawal from the public gaze.

Considering the rush for tickets, the machines are worked accurately. Any fraction over on the divi-dend, such as twopence or a halfpenny, is retained by the club. If the dividend was £1 10s. 2½d., the club would retain the 2½d. I have been inside the machines when in full work, so know exactly how they are managed. I recollect on one race at Eagle Farm a winner was disqualified, and the second horse got the stakes, and of course the totalisator paid over it. It was amusing to see people who had taken tickets on the second horse and torn them up hunting eagerly about the paddock for the pieces. The totalisator, however, does not pay over mutilated tickets. It is a bad plan to tear up a ticket until you know for certain there is no chance of its being negotiable.

Some owners have a way of avoiding publicity when putting money on the machine, and they accomplish it in this way. They find out someone who knows one of the men working the machine. This individual is entrusted with, say £20, to put on a certain horse. He goes up to the ticket-window in good time, before there is a crush on, takes one ticket, which is duly rung on, and hands the £20 to the man inside, whispering him to slip the other nineteen on one at a time when business is brisk, so that it will not be noticed. The other tickets are kept by the clerk inside the machine, who pays out on them after the race, if the horse wins, and no doubt gets a bit for the trouble he has taken. Of course if the £20 had been put on in bulk someone would have noticed it and followed suit, and the dividend would have been materially lessened.

Ten years ago totalisators were run in various shops in Brisbane. This was illegal, but no notice was taken of it for some considerable time. All that is done away with now; but I well remember when big races down South were on, Mooney's and Nesbitt's shops were filled with an excited throng for hours

before the result of the Derby, or the Caulfield or
Melbourne Cup arrived. These shop totalisators were
conducted with fairness, and the promoters merely
took out a percentage, the same as the Race Club.

I was in Mooney's shop when the result of Grace
Darling's Caulfield Cup came in, and it was amusing
to see the look of blank astonishment on the faces of
the people. The mare was a rank outsider, and only
a ticket or two had been taken on her on the off-
chance of getting a big dividend.

These were stirring days in Brisbane, and there
were heaps of money in circulation then. However,
law and the "Puritans" did away with these things,
and about the same time prosperity commenced to
wane, and a terrible dull time fell upon the Northern
Colony.

In the previous chapter I made mention of
"double event" shops in Sydney.

Previous to their establishment totalisators were
run in these places, which, for short, were called "tote
shops," and the men who ran them "tote" proprietors.

It was surprising to what an extent these places,
at one time, existed in Sydney, and for some years
men made fortunes at the game without being
molested. Most of these men adopted names for their
"totes," such as "Leger," "Maori," "Sportsman,"
or the name of some popular racehorse.

" Leger " had about the biggest business in this line, and I have seen a crowd outside his old place in King Street that fairly blocked the road up.

This " tote," and one or two more, were conducted fairly, but the bulk of them were rank swindles, and the dividends declared were false.

The evil became so great that the police were at last reluctantly compelled to prosecute. One " tote " man informed me that it cost him a large sum every week to " square " certain people, and I quite believe him.

Informers were set to work—men who took tickets and then gave information to the police; but it took a long time to stamp them out, and this was not wholly accomplished when I left Sydney. Some enormous dividends were occasionally paid on the straight " totes." As, for instance, over £50 in one place for an investment of 10s.—when Correze ran third in Carbine's Cup. As a rule, however, these big dividends on outsiders were appropriated by the " tote " runners, who, if the public had not backed the horse, put a few tickets on for themselves, after they knew the result.

Thousands of pounds went through the hands of these men in the course of a month, and one successful " tote " man assured me when he dropped the business he had made over £20,000 fairly and squarely in percentages. As he had been at it some years

without being molested, I have no doubt his state-
ment was correct.

The "double event" betting has taken the place
of these "totes," and some curious dodges these men
get up to.

For instance, there is a double on the Flying
Handicap and Farm Handicap at Warwick Farm on a
Saturday.

The names of the horses in the Flying Handicap
are on the top of a card; if there are twenty horses,
there are twenty cards, one for each, and the names
of the horses in the Farm Handicap are printed on
each card below the name of each horse in the Flying
Handicap. As the double is taken the name of the
horse selected is struck out. Say the name of the
horse at the top of the card is Heather. Perhaps a
backer fancies Heather and Winker. If so Winker's
name is struck out on the card with Heather at the
top.

The bookmaker stands in with someone connected
with Heather, and if Heather and Winker is a popular
double, when a backer has taken Winker the card is
quietly pulled down and a clean one, with Winker's
name on, put up. In this manner the double of
Heather and Winker, which is readily snapped up, is
laid, perhaps, some hundreds of times. The bookmaker knows he is perfectly safe, as Heather will not
run. This is a swindle, but only one of many the poor

deluded backer has to put up with. I have seen this done, and on mentioning the fact to the layer was told—

"It's none of your business. If it comes off I'll pay it."

He knew very well there was no earthly chance of its coming off. As for it being none of my business, I thought it was, and to open the eyes of the public I exposed the dodge in the columns of the *Sydney Referee*, the turf department of which I controlled for some years.

Mr. George Adams is the largest and oldest consultation runner in New South Wales, or, for the matter of that, anywhere else.

He runs his consultations, or sweeps, under the name of "Tattersall," and they are very popular all over the Colonies.

Hundreds of thousands of pounds have passed through his hands in these sweeps, which are always drawn on the fairest principle, and in the presence of the press and other people.

He held over two hundred thousand pounds over one Melbourne Cup alone, one consultation being for £100,000 in £1 tickets, and it filled easily. I am writing from memory, but I think the man who drew the first horse received about £25,000, or near it. What a nice haul for a man for an investment of £1.

A glance at the list of winners shows the prizes

are won by all sorts of people in all parts of the Colonies.

When Carbine won, some Chinaman, I believe, in Thursday Island, drew first prize, and the Heathen Chinee, be it said, is generally lucky in his racecourse gambles. When Glenloth won the Cup, a shearer named Layton, in Queensland, drew the horse, and never knew it until the race was over.

When he was apprised of the fact that he was a rich man, he took a couple of mates with him and came to Sydney to draw his money. Being a Scotchman he was canny, and cabled the bulk of it home to his native land. However, he kept enough to have a high old time in Sydney before he set sail, and he gave each of his mates a nice little cheque. He bought a farm in Scotland, and may be there now for all I know.

A cabman in Sydney drew a big winner, and at once handed over his horse and cab as a gift to a mate, and proceeded to go round the world and see things a bit. A policeman drew a big prize, and was so elated that he gave up the ghost, his luck being too much for him. I was never affected that way myself.

An old navvy, working on the railway line in Melbourne, drew a few thousands, but the poor old chap was run over by a train before he could enjoy it.

Mr. H. Oxenham also runs these big consultations, and his name should command no end of support.

Mr. W. R. Wilson, of St. Albans, has entrusted
Mr. Adams to run his big estate and racehorses as a
consultation for £130,000, the first prize being the
St. Albans estate, and Trenton, Carnage, Strathmore, Wallace, and other horses are included in the
prize list. Mr. Adams also ran a big lottery for the
Bank of Van Diemen's Land, various large properties being offered in Hobart as prizes. It is really
surprising how the money rolls in by thousands for
these sweeps and consultations. It shows what money
there is in circulation, and what an immense number
of people are inclined for a quiet gamble. Owners of
horses generally demand a cut out of the sweep from
the man who is fortunate enough to draw a horse.

Some men are grasping in this respect, and demand the lion's share. It is a species of blackmailing
that is detestable. If the drawer of the horse does
not part up, then the owner threatens to scratch his
animal, and sooner than lose all chance of a win the
drawer generally lays a large slice of the sweep.

Some owners would scorn to do such dirty actions,
and I know Mr. W. R. Wilson declined an offer of
part of a sweep about one of his horses, but agreed to
take so much of it as a wager.

The names of the drawers of horses in sweeps are
not supposed to be divulged, but they generally come
out in some way or other, very often through the
fault of the holder of the ticket, who is so overjoyed

at drawing a horse that he must impart the good news
to some of his friends.

The Government of New South Wales have pro-
hibited the delivery of letters containing sweep money,
so that Mr. Adams and Mr. Oxenham have taken
their sweep department to Brisbane, where the Government are not so particular.

This move has cost the postal department of New
South Wales many thousands of pounds a year, as
every letter containing sweep money was registered,
and at a busy time hundreds of such letters were
delivered to "Tattersall."

The Queensland Government will reap all this extra
income, and no doubt they are thankful for small
mercies.

CHAPTER VII.

SOME DERBY AND CUP REMINISCENCES.

Bravo's win. Long odds. A thousand to one. Dreadnought. A short double. A sensational horse. Malvolio. A couple of good ones. That saddle. Glenloth's year. An awful day. The waiter and his sov. Real bad luck.

To chronicle all I have seen on the turf in Australia would fill two or three volumes. It is not my intention to make this book a record of racing since 1884, and I shall merely give reminiscences and incidents likely to interest the reader.

When Bravo won the Melbourne Cup in 1889, I was much interested in the fate of a horse called Chicago. He was a real good horse, and a Caulfield Cup winner; but, somehow, I managed to back him in the wrong race.

When I arrived in Melbourne that year one of the first men I met was the late Mr. Chapman, "Augur," of the *Australasian*. He was a real good fellow, and he told me he had backed Bravo to win at the forlorn odds of a thousand to one.

.5

It appears some rash bookmaker, more in a spirit of bravado than anything else, had offered to lay a thousand pounds to a sov. against Bravo, and "Augur" had stood in with a friend to the extent of £250 worth to a dollar.

Bravo had been reported so lame that his starting was regarded as out of the question. A few days before the race Bravo came into the market again, and was well backed. The bookmakers who had been taking liberties with him felt uneasy, and a lot of the money they had laid against him at long odds was hedged at a loss.

The Melbourne Stakes on the Saturday had produced a terrific race between Abercorn, Melos, and Carbine, who passed the post in that order.

Abercorn, on that day, was at his best, and I never saw him run a better race. At this particular time he was even better than Carbine, but it must not be forgotten that the son of Musket had one of his fore-hoofs tightly bound up, and was not at his best.

Before the race for the Stakes, a well-known bank manager came to me and asked me what I thought would win the Derby, and I said it was a good thing for Dreadnought; but as the odds were three to one *on*, it was like buying money.

He then asked what I thought would win the Stakes, and I said it ought to be a great race between Abercorn and Carbine. He then said he could get

three to one against the double—Abercorn for the
Stakes and Dreadnought for the Derby.

A terribly short price to take about a double; but,
after all, it did not look so bad when I reckoned up
that if Abercorn won he would have three to one
against Dreadnought—a certainty if ever there was
one—instead of having to lay three to one on him. On
my advice he took the wager to a fair amount, and I
stood in. I was precious glad when the Stakes' race
was over, and it was touch and go. Abercorn, however, won, and we had a rosy bet of three to one
against Dreadnought, who simply won the Derby as
he liked, after his stable mate, Rudolph, had made all
the running for him.

Dreadnought was a good horse, a chestnut; but
after he was sold at Mr. White's sale, he turned out
not worth his purchase-money.

I think it was at this time Mr. Brodribb commenced his desperate plunges on the turf. One of his
freaks was giving over four thousand guineas for a
gelding called Titan, by Chester, bred by Mr. White.
Titan, as a two-year-old, was a wonder, and at the top
of the tree. The Derby looked a certainty for him
when Mr. Brodribb bought him, but the horse went
all wrong. As a matter of fact, I do not think Titan
ever won him a race, and he was sold to Mr. Donald
Wallace for a few hundreds. Changing hands again
appeared at first to have done Titan very little good;

but when Mr. Wallace had had him for some time, he came on wonderfully, and won several good races. Titan developed into a remarkably fine horse, and the last time I saw him at Randwick, before his death, he was about the best-looking horse in the paddock.

Titan won the Toorak Handicap at Caulfield a couple of years back, and I have cause to remember that win, as he beat Mr. Oatley's horse, Bel Giorno, trained by Mr. W. Forrester. In Bel Giorno Mr. Forrester thought he had a good thing for this race, and he told me to back it before he left Sydney. Titan, however, beat him after a capital finish; but I had my revenge when Warpaint just beat Titan on the last day of the meeting.

Warpaint I secured the good odds of ten to one about, and although I think Titan was unlucky to lose, the win was none the less welcome.

Titan followed his Caulfield success up with an easy win at Flemington with a heavy weight in the saddle, and Mr. O'Brien remarked to me after that race that a Newmarket handicap had been thrown away with the son of Chester. Had Mr. Wallace kept Titan for the Newmarket, he would have got in with not much over eight stone, and the race would, I think, have been little short of a certainty for him. So much for the sensational Titan.

Bravo's Cup win was not such a surprise as many people imagined, for the horse was well backed at

twelve to one on the day of the race. He beat Carbine and Melos, who finished in that order. After his
forward running in the Stakes, Melos was naturally a
great favourite, as he had a lot less weight to carry.
Bravo's win put a good stake into the pocket of his
owner, Mr. W. T. Jones, of Ballarat, a good racing
man, with plenty of money at his back.

Next year's Cup was won by Carbine; but that
event I will leave for the present, as a special chapter
is devoted to this great horse.

In 1891, Malvolio, by Malua—Madcap, won the
Cup, beating Sir William and Strathmore.

Malvolio was bred by Mr. Redfearn, who trained
him, and was ridden to victory by his son. Mr. James
Redfearn is a trainer well up in his business, and a
jolly good fellow to boot, and the victory of his horse
was popular, although had Sir William got home, it
would have pleased the Sydney people better. Sir
William was a handsome horse, and trained by Mr. E.
Keys, and had the advantage of Jack Fielder in the
saddle. The astute "Teddy" fancied he had a real
good thing in Sir William, and the result proved he
was not far out. Had Sir William got home, I know
one or two men who would have been many thousands of pounds richer.

Strathmore won the Derby that year, and of course
was heavily backed for the Cup, as the Derby winner
almost invariably is. Strathmore was a remarkably

good horse, and he had a bad run in the Cup, or I think he would have been nearer. Some people go so far as to say he would have beaten Malvolio; but this I cannot agree with. Mr. Forrester always maintains that Highborn finished third in this race, and so I thought. However, the black fellow ran well enough with his weight to show he was a good horse at a distance.

Mr. McCulloch, the judge, told me in Scott's, next morning, that it was a case of neck and neck for third place in this race, but Strathmore just beat Highborn in the last stride. That last stride did Highborn's owner out of a thousand for third money, and also sundry place bets. Although Malvolio was a good horse, I never had much fancy for him after his Cup win, and it must have taken a lot out of him.

There was some trouble about paying over the stakes in this race. Mr. E. de Mestre put in a claim for them, on the ground that he owned Madcap, the dam of Malvolio, and had merely lent her to Mr. Redfearn. This Mr. Redfearn denied; and I think Mr. de Mestre was ill-advised to make the claim he did. Malvolio's owner got the stakes, and rightly so.

Three very sensational Cups followed this win of Malvolio's, and, as a rule, there is plenty of excitement over a Melbourne Cup.

In 1892 Camoola won the Derby. He was a hot favourite; but the result proved he had not so much in hand as his backers fancied, for he rolled a lot at the finish, and Huxley had to handle him carefully. He was trained by Mr. Tom Payten, who also had another good colt that year in Autonomy. Mr. Payten mystified the horse watchers on the Flemington track in the early morning with the doings of Camoola and Autonomy. Both were in the Derby, and naturally there was a desire to find out which colt would carry the stable confidence in that race. They were generally galloped together. One morning, Autonomy would beat Camoola badly; two mornings after, Camoola would leave Autonomy far behind. All this was most annoying to the people who imagine other people's business ought to be theirs. I fancy the trainer must have had the heavy saddle changed occasionally.

There is a story attached to this saddle. It is reported that on one occasion, when the painters were doing up the saddle-room at Newmarket, one of the men asked a stable lad to remove an innocent-looking saddle on one of the trees.

The lad, without a thought, pulled it down by the stirrup-leather, in order to catch it. When it fell, this saddle nearly broke the youngster's neck, for it weighed about *four stone*.

Mr. Payten may smile at this yarn; but Tom generally has "a bit up his sleeve" in his trial gallops. I fancy his "sleeve" must have been full up a week or two before Projectile romped in for the Metropolitan Stakes at Randwick.

Camoola, as I said before, won the Derby and Autonomy landed the Stakes the same day. Much diversity of opinion existed as to whether Camoola or Automony was the better colt. I preferred Autonomy myself for any distance up to a mile and a half; and from the way he won the Stakes, I think he would have won the Derby easier than Camoola. He was a beautiful bay horse, and Camoola a chestnut, with lop ears, and a peculiarly laboured style of galloping, just for all the world like a horse pumped out after a hard race. Both, however, were rattling good horses, but very unlucky after their three-year-old careers.

What an awful Cup it was this year. I have been at race-meetings in all sorts of weather in the old country and elsewhere, but I never recollect a more uncomfortable day than when Glenloth won the Cup. Torrents of rain came down and deluged everybody, and turned the course into a quagmire at the far side. All the fashionable world turned out as usual. Nothing short of an earthquake would prevent Melbourne people going to the Cup, and even then, if the course was clear, they would sit on the ruins of the stands and watch the race.

The lawn became very slippery, and it was amusing to see the numerous spills, as some well-dressed swell measured his length in the mud, and then got up to shake himself like a Newfoundland dog.

This year Mr. Forrester had two horses in the race, Ronda and Penance, and the former had done a good trial. In the Trial Stakes, however, on the first day, Ronda was beaten, which did not make his Cup chance look rosy. Nasty remarks were made about his performance in this race after the Cup; but they were uncalled-for, as the stable lost a lot of money over him in the Trial Stakes. Penance had run Carbine a great race as a two-year old, but had never run up to that form since. However, he was well handicapped. I think that set-to with Carbine knocked all the pluck out of him, and no wonder, for it was a terrible task to set a two-year-old to beat him.

The rain poured down like a second deluge when the horses came out. The mud flew up in a shower in the preliminary canter, and in the actual race it can easily be imagined what it was like.

I was in the press box on the top of the Grand Stand, and at the back of this, some distance away, is "the hill," which was crowded with a wet, miserable mass of people.

Umbrellas were put up by some people on the top of the stand, but loud shouts from the crowd on the hill ordered them to be shut. Many declined to close their umbrellas, and a shower of mud in lumps came rattling down on them from the irate crowd on the hill. This had the desired effect.

On the flat there was a perfect forest of umbrellas, and it was a strange sight as seen from our box. As for seeing the race, it was well nigh impossible, and when the horses flashed past the post there was a cry of " What's won ? "

When Glenloth's number went up it put the finishing touch on backers' misery, as the horse was a rank outsider, and fifty to one could have been had about him in places.

Ronda finished second and Penance third, so that Mr. Forrester's bad luck in this race still stuck to him. In three years he had with his horses run second, fourth, and second and third, not a bad record.

An incident that happened over this race shows how unwise it is to put a man off backing a horse when he fancies it.

Before I left my hotel in the morning, one of the waiters asked me to put him a pound on Glenloth. I laughed at him, and told him to keep his money in his pocket. He did, with the result that he was about £50 worse off after Glenloth won, as he would have procured that amount to his pound.

I shall never forget the mournful look with which he regarded me after that event. I had serious thoughts of changing my table, in case a concoction

of arsenic fell into the soup by mistake. Thinking
to make matters better, I advised him to back Trieste
in the Oaks.   He did, and she lost, but she ought to
have won, which only made matters worse.

Moral : Always keep your information to yourself,
and then you will be the only sufferer.

Glenloth was a good stamp of horse, but the wet
day was all in his favour.   He might have won under
any circumstances, but the heavy going assisted a
horse of his build.

Robson rode him, but the victory did not do him
much good.   Strange to say, many jockeys that win
the Cup meet with bad luck afterwards, some
through no fault of their own.

CHAPTER VIII.

THE year following Glenloth's wet Cup I once more
found myself in Melbourne for the two big meetings
at Caulfield and Flemington.

We generally went overland from Sydney to Melbourne, and some fun we had when we got a merry
party together in the Pullman car. The journey by
train from Sydney to Melbourne is about five hundred
miles. The express leaves Sydney at 5.15 p.m. and
reaches Melbourne next day at 11.30 a.m. The sleeping cars are models of comfort, and the journey is
made as pleasant as possible for travellers.

When first I travelled this journey there was a
vexatious delay at Albury, the border town between

New South Wales and Victoria, where we had to change from the Sydney into the Melbourne train. This has to be done because the gauge of the railway lines is different. Eight or nine years ago they were very particular in examining baggage, as the duties were heavy on certain articles. It seems a monstrous thing that it should be necessary to search passengers' luggage merely because they pass out of one Colony into another. It is an absurdity, and so most travellers thought it.

On the return journey from Melbourne, in 1891, we had an alarm of fire on the train. Lord Jersey, the Governor, was in a special car behind ours. The attendant roused me, and said, " There's a fire, sir ! You'd better get out ! "

" No, you don't," I replied. " It's not time to turn out yet."

The attendant has a knack of rousing you up early in order to make up the beds in the car. I fancied his fire alarm was a happy inspiration on his part to get me out.

When I saw people hurrying out of the car, and the train had stopped, I felt it was time to make a move. A sudden thought occurred to me. I felt I could earn undying fame as a staunch supporter of our great Empire, so I sang out, " Save the Governor."

An old Scotchman was in the berth over mine, and

he growled out, "Save the Governor, be d——d. Where's *me boots?*"

Evidently the gentleman from the North did not coincide with my views. He wished to make tracks.

Happily no great harm was done, only one side of the car had been burnt through some of the rods being overheated. An amusing account of the incident appeared in a Melbourne paper, *Bohemian.* Here is the extract which I happened to come across :—

"The true story of that fire on board the Sydney express, about a week ago, has not yet been told. The alleged origin of the outbreak that nearly devoured the new Pullman car and its contents, may pass for what it is worth ; but no one has yet ventured to describe the scene in the interior of the car after the alarm was sounded. The alarm of 'fire,' when uttered in a shrill voice in the small hours of the morning, never fails to have the desired effect on the soundest sleeper, especially if the cry be uttered by a female. On this occasion it had the desired effect on every soul in the carriage. A lady who slept in a berth near the door heard it first, and, running out into the passage that traverses the carriage, in her *robe de nuit,* was confronted by the stalwart figure of Dibbs, the new Premier, who was vainly attempting to find his way into the trousers of Nat Gould, the author of 'The Double Event.' Nat is fat and short, and Dibbs is a big fellow, and slim; with an altitude of 6 feet 3 inches. When the alarm was given, Gould promptly seized hold of Dibbs' clothes, and made straight for the open air. By the time Dibbs got his eyes open there was only one pair of trousers available, and they were Gould's. When he met the hysterical female in curl papers, the New South Wales Premier had only got one leg into Gould's unmentionables, but he struggled manfully to cover the other with a newspaper. Gould's plight was even worse ; he had got his legs into the sleeves of Dibbs' shooting-jacket, and, when discovered out on the line a few minutes later by the guard, he was carrying over his arm a set of lady's overalls, which he had borne off triumphantly in his flight."

Such is the account given by a smart man of this memorable episode.

I may as well state here that I have never been much troubled with railway accidents. The only one, bar the fire, was on returning from Newcastle races to Sydney. I was in the front carriage with several trainers and one or two jockeys. A neat little game at Nap was going on, when suddenly there was a jolt and a cry, " We're off the line ! " A portmanteau and a saddle were deposited on my head, and I felt the seat underneath me giving way.

It was a nasty five minutes, but luckily the engine, which had gone off the line and fallen into a gully, had lodged somehow, and the tender propped our carriage up and stopped the train going over the bank.

It was a narrow squeak as we saw when we had scrambled out through the windows, the doors being jammed so that we could not open them.

No sooner had we discovered all danger was over than we saw one of our party climbing back into the carriage, bent upon securing "Kitty" and any stray Nap coins.

The Cup following Glenloth's was won by another outsider—Tarcoola—and again I had a bad time, as I backed Carnage for the double—the Derby and Cup. Carnage won the Derby all right, but just failed in the Cup, as he ran second, after making nearly all the running. It was an extraordinary performance on the part of a three-year-old, as early in the season as November, to make nearly the whole of the pace in a two-mile race, and then just get beaten. It was about as good a performance as I ever saw a three-year-old do in November.

But I am anticipating. Tarcoola was trained by Mr. Joe Cripps, and ran in his name, and, as in the case of Malvolio, was ridden by the son of the trainer. Mr. Greenaway was the owner of Tarcoola for some time, and the horse lost him a heap of money. He told me it nearly made him throw up racing when he saw Tarcoola land such a stake as the Melbourne Cup after he had sold him.

It is curious how men sometimes miss a good win.

One morning I was coming off the track with Mr. Frank Wilkinson, a well-known pressman and handicapper, when he turned round and said, "Stop a minute, Nat; here's Tarcoola going for a spin."

"Hang Tarcoola," I said. "I'm in a hurry for breakfast."

Frank had, however, got his watch on them, and I waited until the gallop was over.

"By Jove! that's a great go," said Frank, looking at his watch. "It's worth taking a few pounds about Tarcoola at 100 to 2 or 3."

I said, "We'll think about it. You can get a bit in the Club, and I'll go you halves."

Unfortunately Frank did not get the money, and a day or two after Tarcoola did such a bad gallop I forgot all about him until I saw him beating my pet fancy, Carnage, in the Cup. I believe Mr. Wilkinson wired the result of the good gallop to a friend in Sydney, who won a thousand over Tarcoola. Such is luck.

Tarcoola won cleverly from Carnage and Jeweller, with Loyalty well up, and again the public were floored, as Tarcoola started at a very long price.

The last Cup I saw, previous to sailing for London, was in 1894, when Patron won. Again an outsider landed the race, and it was a most extraordinary victory, as I will endeavour to show.

6

Patron was a very good three-year-old, and naturally he was backed early in the season for the Cup. On paper his chance looked as good as anything in the race. Some of the first double-event wagers booked were for Paris in the Caulfield Cup and Patron in the Melbourne Cup. Before the date for the Cup arrived Patron went wrong, and his name gradually receded in the betting-list until, shortly before the race, long odds could have been had about his chance. Paris won the Caulfield Cup, and a well-known jockey—I will not mention names—had the double, Paris and Patron. So confident, however, was he that Patron could not win, from information received, that he hedged the whole of his Patron money to two book-makers. Dawes, the jockey who rode Patron, had not much faith in his mount, and Mr. Purchas, the owner, laid off as much of his money as he could. I believe that even as late as the evening before the race, it was not decided whether Patron should run or be scratched. This was certainly not encouraging for anyone who had backed him. It was, however, decided to start the horse and let him take his chance, and, much to the surprise of nearly everyone, he won after a good race with Devon and Nada. The latter was in Mr. Wilson's stable, and was backed for a heap of money. She had done a good trial at St. Alban's, and she evidently ran up to it.

Devon was the unlucky horse of the season. He

won the Toorak Handicap at Caulfield, and thereby earned a penalty for the Caulfield Cup, or he would have won it for a certainty. As it was he crossed his legs at a critical part of the race, and was beaten on the post by Paris. Devon followed this up by running second in the Melbourne Cup, and a few days after he ran again second to Taranaki in the Williamstown Cup. It was very bad luck indeed to run three seconds in such important races.

The jockey before alluded to, who had the double —Paris and Patron—actually backed Devon in the Melbourne Cup with the money he drew over Patron. If that was not the devil's own luck I don't think it could be very well beaten.

The Harvester, a colt owned by Mr. Sam Cook, the trainer, who bred him, I think, won the Derby. There was a lot of bumping at the finish of the race, and an objection was laid against the winner. Bonnie Scotland, who ran third, had a bad run; but I think the stewards were right in not disturbing the judge's verdict. Chris Moore rode the winner, and was naturally very anxious about the result. The stewards were considering the matter long after the last race had been run, and it was a curious sight to see the bars lighted with candles, and the racecourse suddenly enveloped in darkness.

I was on the lawn with Mr. Forrester, Mr. James Redfearn, and Mr. John McLoughlin, of Sydney, and to kill time I offered to run Mr. Forrester a hundred yards for a "bottle of cham." I fancy the spurt I gave induced Mr. Forrester to think I could run, and he forfeited. I can assure him the spurt I gave took it all out of me, so it was lucky for me he did not toe the scratch. When it was known The Harvester had got the race, we four left the course in a waggonette, and after sundry adventures on the road reached Scott's Hotel, where I believe we had a very fair night of it. Mr. John McLoughlin was a worthy lawyer of Sydney —a real good sort, and very fond of a racehorse. In Correze he had a good one, but the horse never seemed to be thoroughly at his best, except when he won the V. R. C. Handicap in the fastest time on record. Mention of Mr. McLoughlin's name reminds me of a little adventure in Sydney. I had been to the theatre, and met Mr. McLoughlin as I came out. He asked me if I was going home, and I said, "Yes." He then proposed I should ride home, as far as I had to go, in his cab.

I agreed, and there he kept me, in the cab, until we reached his house at Bronte, miles beyond where I wanted to alight.

I remained for supper, then had a stroll round the grounds—it was a beautiful moonlight night—and then a peep at Correze. He had the horse stabled at his house then. I reached home about 2·0 a.m., and it took all my persuasive powers to convince my good wife I had been the victim of Mr. McLoughlin's little scheme. "All's well that ends well," and I was none the worse for keeping such late hours.

I have mentioned Paris before, and his numerous victories are fresh in my mind. The game little son of Grandmaster is now in England, and Mr. John Allsop's brother brought him over.

Paris won his first Caulfield Cup in 1892, and followed it up with a win in 1894. Cis Parker rode him on the first occasion, and Jack Fielder on the second. Both were good races, but his second win was a brilliant performance in such a big field, and with his heavy weight—nine-stone four.

When he won the Metropolitan Stakes at Randwick he started at 100 to 3, and won gallantly. Over a mile few horses could beat him, and he is a thorough stayer as well. I never saw a horse that could equal him on the track, and morning after morning he used to do the fastest gallop of any horse out. He was certainly one of the very best horses I saw in the Colonies.

In 1893 the Caulfield Cup proved sensational. Tim Swiveller won, with Sainfoin second, and Oxide third. An objection was laid against Tim Swiveller on the ground of interference, and Chris Moore rode him.

The Caulfield stewards decided not to interfere, and the race was given to Tim Swiveller. The owner

of Sanfoin then appealed to the V. R. C. as he had a
perfect right to do.

Much to the surprise of the ring, and racing men
generally, the V. R. C. awarded the race to Sanfoin, disqualified Tim Swiveller, and placed Oxide
second. This was very hard luck for the Hon. Geo.
Davis, the owner of Tim Swiveller, and he was not
the sort of man to let the affair rest, for he defended
his case admirably. It seems a remarkable thing
that the verdict of such a body of stewards as at
Caulfield, who saw the race officially, should be over-
ruled by the V. R. C., who did not see the race
officially. That Tim Swiveller interfered with Sanfoin
I have very little doubt, as I saw the race, and had a
splendid view of the finish. The horse, however, that
suffered most was Oxide. He got jammed between
Tim Swiveller and Sanfoin, and Cis Parker, his rider,
had to pull up his head or he would probably have
been down. I do not believe Chris Moore, the
rider of Tim Swiveller, wilfully did anything wrong.
His mount was a horse that used to hang a lot
at the finish of a race, and this caused him to bore
in.

A photograph taken of the finish of the race was,
I believe, the main point upon which the V. R. C.
based their decision. It is said the photographic appa-
ratus cannot lie, but I have seen photos of people
very unlike them, so there must be something wrong

somewhere. I am not much of a believer in the photo evidence in cases of this kind.

Sanfoin getting the stakes made a vast difference to the ring, and there was a lot of grumbling over the matter.

CHAPTER IX.

CARBINE AND HIS CUP.

A great racehorse. His Cup win. Some interesting particulars. On board the " Orizaba." The voyage to England. Mr. Ernest Day. His yarns. A successful trip. A letter from Mr. Forrester. Carbine does him out of £28,000. Narrow shave for a fortune.

IN the preceding chapters I have omitted the Melbourne Cup won by Carbine in 1890, as I think the horse is worthy of a chapter to himself; he was the best racehorse I ever saw during my residence in Australia. Carbine, by Musket—Mersey, was bred in New Zealand, and purchased as a yearling by Mr. Dan O'Brien for 620 guineas. His performances, when they come to be carefully considered, are wonderful. The horse won thirty-three out of forty-three races in which he started, and was only out of a place once, and he was then suffering from a cracked heel. He won fifteen races in succession, and eighteen races out of twenty, being unluckily second in the two he lost.

As a two-year-old he ran five times in New Zealand, and won each race. He was brought over by his owner to Victoria to run for the V. R. C. Derby in 1888, and was unluckily second to Ensign. He ran third in the Newmarket Handicap to Sedition, a rank outsider, and that good horse, Lochiel; and in the Australian Cup, 2¼ miles, he was beaten by Lochiel, who carried 8st. 7lb. to Carbine's 8st. 6lb.—a real good performance for a three-year-old.

He won the Champion Stakes, 3 mile, as a three-year-old, beating Abercorn, who was then a four-year-old, at w. f. a. He won several races this season, including the Sydney Cup, in which he carried 9st., or within 4lbs. of Abercorn, who finished third. This race goes far to prove he was a better horse than Abercorn, as he was receiving only 4lbs. and giving away a year.

As a four-year-old he ran second to Bravo in the Melbourne Cup, with 10st. on his back, giving the winner 1st. 7lb. He again won the Sydney Cup, carrying 9st. 9lb.—a race the handicapper treated him too leniently in. It was in the Canterbury Plate at the V. R. C. meeting he ran the only unplaced during the whole of his career. Space will not permit of me giving all his wins, but I can safely say he held the championship as a w. f. a. horse from three years old until he retired from the turf. He beat all the best horses over all distances, and he was as good at seven furlongs or a mile as he was at two or three miles. In

these days of sprinters and non-stayers, it is a treat to
see a horse of such grand speed and staying powers
combined as Carbine.

It was as a four-year-old Carbine performed the
great feat of winning five of the principal races at the
A. J. C. Autumn Meeting in four days, including the
Sydney Cup and four w. f. a. races.

No wonder Dan O'Brien heaved a sigh, for he had
sold Carbine to Mr. Donald Wallace for 3000 guineas
some time before. It was a treat to see the way in
which Carbine tackled his opponents. The horse
fairly revelled in his work, and his rush at the finish
was marvellous. I have never seen a horse of his size
cover so much ground in his stride.

If Carbine was a wonder up to four years old, what
shall we say for his five-year-old career, which fairly
eclipsed all that he had previously done. He ran
eleven times, and was beaten once, when he ought to
have won. He won his memorable Melbourne Cup
this season, and about it I have something of interest
to relate.

I had special opportunities of learning a good deal
more about that race before it came off than most
people. Mr. William Forrester, of Warwick Farm, had
in his stable a horse called Highborn that he had specially kept for this event. Mr. Forrester was then,
and, I am proud to say, still is, a great friend of mine;
and I also knew Mr. Hickenbotham, the trainer of

Carbine, very well. I went to Warwick Farm from Sydney, about an hour's ride in the train, to have a peep at the horses. Warwick Farm is a snug place, and the house and stables join on to Mr. Oatley's private racecourse. Mr. Forrester is brimful of hospitality, and a born gentleman if ever there was one. When we came to Highborn's box, Mr. Forrester said, " What do you think of him? "

I was looking at a lanky, flat-sided common gelding, as black as coal, with a wall eye that made him look wicked. Honestly, I could not say I thought much of him. It was wonderful how he improved upon acquaintance. " He's no beauty," I replied, or words to that effect.

Mr. Forrester smiled, and gave me to understand if I did not have a few pounds on " the black fellow " in the Melbourne Cup I should regret it. Knowing "the Squire's" propensity for practical joking, I thought he was trying it on, but I soon found out he was serious. He had specially kept Highborn for this particular race, and when the weights came out with Carbine 10st. 5lb. and Highborn 6st. 8lb., there was much joy in the Warwick Farm camp. The preparation of both horses went on satisfactorily, but Carbine's trainer had a lot of trouble with the horse's feet, and had a very anxious time of it. Mr. Forrester and some of his friends were quietly putting money on Highborn at very long odds months before the race. Highborn's trial was good enough to win with nearer 9st. up than 6st. 8lb., so no wonder they were sanguine. When I reached Melbourne that year for the Cup meeting, I saw Carbine do his winding-up preparations on the track at Flemington. One morning he beat his stable mate, Megaphone—for whom Mr. Wallace had given 2,000 guineas or more after he ran Carbine such a great race at Randwick—badly. Meeting Mr. Hickenbotham after the gallop, I remarked what a good go it was.

" Yes," he replied, " and weight or no weight, bar accidents, he'll win the Cup." I had an idea he could go near it, but doubted if he could give 3st. 11lb. to a horse like Highborn. About a week before the Melbourne Cup was run, I met Mr. Forrester, and he asked me to go up to Oakleigh Park, as they were going to give Highborn a run there. I went, to my sorrow, for Highborn was just beaten by Mr. James Redfearn's Malvolio. I remarked to Mr. Forrester, after the race, that a beating like that was not good enough to win a Melbourne Cup.

" Don't make any mistake," was his reply. " Malvolio's Redfearn's crack three-year-old, and he'll win the next Melbourne Cup with him." Sure enough his words came true, for I saw Malvolio win it the following year.

But to the race. When the saddling bell rang before the Cup race there was intense excitement, and Carbine held his position as favourite firm as a rock, and Highborn was at 33 to 1. Ramage rode Carbine, and Egan, a tiny lad, Highborn. "Old Jack" was fairly nobbled as he was being saddled, but as usual he took no notice of the crowd. When he came on to the track there was a terrific burst of cheering. Carbine stood still and looked round, and then declined to go to the post. Mr. Hickenbotham gave him a push behind, and Carbine moved a few paces. This was a slow process. At last Ramage threw the reins over the horse's head, and Mr. Hickenbotham fairly dragged him up the course. I never saw a more sluggish horse until he commenced to race, and then there was a different tale to tell. Mr. Forrester was very confident Highborn would beat him.

I shall never forget that race. Carbine held a good position throughout, but did not get well to the front until they were in the straight. At the home turn Highborn looked to have a chance second to none, and the hopes of his backers were high. No sooner, however, did Carbine see an opening than he shot through, and after that it was a case of hare and hounds. On came "Old Jack," with his 10st. 5lb., and at the distance he had the race won. Cheer after cheer rent the air, and people went almost frantic with excitement. It was a wild scene. For months Carbine had been backed by the public, and at last the suspense was over. It was a glorious victory, and everyone knew it, but none better than Mr. Forrester, whose crack Highborn finished a couple of lengths behind him. Not only did Carbine carry 10st. 5lb., but he ran the two miles in 3 min. 28¼ secs., the fastest time on record for that distance in the Colonies.

To show how good the performance was, I have only to allude to Highborn's performances afterwards. Highborn won the Australian Cup, the Sydney Cup, and the Anniversary Handicap, and ran fourth in the Melbourne Cup the following year with 9st. up. He was sold to go to India, and when the property of the Maharajah of Cooch Behar he won two Viceroy's Cups in succession.

A word as to Carbine's defeat by Marvel at Randwick. It was a wet day, and the ground was sticky. In the All Aged Stakes, a mile, Carbine ran without plates and could obtain no hold. It was pitiable to see him floundering and not able to stretch out in his usual grand style. The same afternoon he met Marvel again in the Cumberland Stakes, two miles. This time Carbine ran in shoes. The race resolved itself into a gallop over the last mile, which was all in favour of Marvel. Carbine, however, beat him badly, and I think there is no doubt he would have won the other race had he had shoes on.

I saw Carbine win all his big races, and when he was bought by the Duke of Portland for £13,000, I came to London in the same vessel he was on, the Orient liner R.M.S. "Orizaba." A few particulars about

Carbine's voyage may be of interest. The horse did not come on board until we reached Melbourne.

Mr. Ernest Day, who had charge of him for the Duke, was naturally very anxious to get the horse shipped quietly. A notice appeared in the *Evening Herald*, on Thursday, stating Carbine would be shipped on Saturday morning. As I happened to have a letter in my pocket stating he would come on board on Good Friday, I smiled. Evidently the paragraph had been inspired to put people off the scent. I was on board when the " hero of a hundred fights " came to the pier, and the horse was accompanied by the colt by Carbine—Novelette, who has been named Lerderderg by the Duke of Portland, and who was alongside of him. " Old Jack " at first seemed inclined to remain ashore. Mr. Day endeavoured to persuade him to step on to the gangway, but he declined the invitation. A handful of clover was given him, which he quietly munched, then he looked at the crowd as much as to say, " What do you think of me ? " Cunningham, the man who has had charge of Carbine at the stud, and who came home with the horses, then went to the rescue. No sooner did Carbine see him coming along the gangway than he stretched out his neck and put one foot forward. Cunningham spoke to him, and then quietly pulling the head-stall, Carbine followed him like a lamb. The horse felt his footing carefully all along the gangway, and crouched down when he felt the boards creak under him; but he never made the least objection to following his leader. Once in his box Carbine commenced to munch hay quietly, as though a trip to England was an everyday occurrence with him. The colt took more trouble to get on board, but once in his box he settled down like an old horse. Not knowing the time Carbine was to go on board, there was not a great crowd there, but on Saturday morning (April 13th, 1895) the people came down in hundreds to have a last peep at the champion. When it was found Carbine had been put on board the day before, the crowd commenced to see they had been sold, but they were determined not to be done out of a sight of him. I never saw a more determined mass of people than Carbine's admirers. They crushed up the gangway and jammed up in front of his box, regardless of torn clothes and pickpockets, and there were plenty of the latter about, or what looked like them. Hundreds of people caught a passing glimpse of Carbine as he stood quietly eating in his box. It was their last sight of "Old Jack," and there were many present who had won money over him in that memorable Melbourne Cup. No horse that ever ran in Australia was a greater idol with the public than Carbine, and the pier was crowded with his admirers long before the boat sailed.

* * * * * *

When we cast off from Sandridge Pier there was a mighty burst of cheering, and cries of "Carbine" rent the air. I was near the horse's box at the time with Mr. Day, and "Old Jack" pricked up his ears and raised his splendid head at the sound, as though he fancied there was another race to be run. A beautiful wreath was sent on board for Carbine. It was in the shape of a horseshoe, and had Donald Wallace's colours on, and written on a card attached to it, "For dear old Carbine; *bon voyage*." Had Carbine got hold of that wreath, I am afraid he would have made short work of it. Mr. Day had several chats with me during the voyage. He is a most entertaining man, and has travelled all over the world in charge of horses. He took a consignment of horses to India for the Ameer of Afghanistan, and safely conveyed them through the famous Khyber Pass. The Ameer's sons came out to meet him, and they were escorted into the capital by a troop of horsemen, whose soldierly bearing made them look exceptionally fierce. The Ameer asked Day how he would accept a gift—in skins or precious stones. Day, with all due respect to his Afghanistan Nibs, said he would prefer gold. The Ameer is reported to have winked the other eye and given Day a cheque on the Bank of India. At all events, Mr. D. got the ready. On another occasion he had to secrete himself in the luggage-

7

waggon of a train and flee from Buenos Ayres
when the revolution was on in that city. Mr. Day
says that bullets pattering on the roof of a house
are not pleasant. He lost £3,000 in the smash-up
that followed, and was glad to return with a whole
skin. At that time he was training for a wealthy
Italian, for whom he had bought a stud of racers
in England, and who lost all he possessed in the
revolution. One morning I went with Mr. Day to
see Carbine have his breakfast. I pulled a few
stalks of green clover out of the bundle and put
them between my teeth. "Old Jack" put his nose
between the bars and took them as gently as though
he had been my particular pal all his life. I never
saw such a quiet, docile stallion, and throughout
the voyage the horse behaved splendidly. At
Colombo Carbine had a narrow escape. The horse
was very ill, and Mr. Day had to perform an
operation on him, which he did successfully, and
no man could have paid more attention to the
horse than he did. Cunningham held the horse's
head during the operation, and Mr. Day happening
to look up saw blood running down his sleeve. On
asking what was the matter, Cunningham said, "Oh,
nothing; Old Jack had a bite at my arm." No
wonder with two such attendants and on board a
steady boat as the "Orizaba" undoubtedly is,
Carbine should have arrived safely.

At Welbeck Carbine will be mated with some of the best mares in the world, and he ought to get good stock from St. Simon mares.

I cannot conclude this chapter in a more fitting manner than by quoting a portion of a letter I received from Mr. W. Forrester since I have been in England, dated Warwick Farm, 6th May. He writes :—

"So you are a mate of Carbine's. Notwithstanding my thinking him the greatest racehorse the world has ever seen, I wish he had never been foaled, as you know he cut me out of £28,400 in the Melbourne Cup. Need I say what a surprise, as I thought I could not lose, when old Carbine was seen with his 10st. 5lb. beating me badly. Had I won that day I feel sure I would have cleared £50,000 over the meeting, as there were Correze and Muriel in the V. R. C. and Free Handicaps that I looked upon as the best of good things, but I was in hobbles and could not have a dash. If Rosary has a colt foal by the old horse it may be a second Carbine. I am glad to tell you she is in foal to him, and should it face the starter it will be known as Fatal Bullet. Could you suggest anything better? (I suggested Battle Abbey, which Mr. Forrester liked very much.) By Chester's brother out of Commotion's sister with Carbine on top, one will be pardoned if he anticipates something

A 1. I have not the slightest doubt he will nick
with the Duke of Portland's mares if they give him
plenty of work and not keep him stalled up like
something one wanted for Smithfield market, and
keep the shoes off him as much as they possibly can,
as most of the stallion's trouble in old age is with
the feet, caused by being continually shod. We let
them live down here without shoes on. Why not in
old England?"

CHAPTER X.

As in every other country all kinds of horses are to be found in Australia, good, bad, and indifferent.

Considering the racehorses are all descended from English blood, often of the best strains, it is not to be wondered at that some good horses are to be found on the turf in the Colonies. To trace back the pedigrees of almost any good horse in Australia is to find the same blood noticeable in the pedigrees of English horses.

With such a climate as Australasia possesses, more especially New Zealand and Tasmania, it would be extraordinary if horses could not be properly bred and reared.

Regarding the respective merits of English and Australian racehorses, it is a difficult matter to decide. I am afraid it will never be possible to thoroughly test

their merits on the racecourse, as the conditions of
climate are all against a true trial, and the voyage is
long and tedious.   The late Hon. James White made
an experiment in sending a couple of yearlings to
England, Kirkham and Narallen, but they turned out
failures.   Ringmaster ran in England and won a few
races.   In the Colonies Ringmaster was a mere pony,
and not a first-class racehorse by any means ; so if he
could score under about similar weights to those he
carried in the Colonies, I think it is an indication that
the best Colonial horses would hold their own in
England.

I am perfectly certain that there are many horses
in Australia that would give the last Derby winner,
Sir Visto, or any of those behind him, a good lump of
weight and beat them.

Again, when Australian and English horses have
met in India, the former have more than held their
own.   Certainly the Indian climate may be more
favourable to Australian horses, although it is very
different to what they have been accustomed to.   Such
horses as Carbine, Abercorn, Marvel, Bungebah, Paris,
Strathmore, Portsea, Boz, Fishwife, William Tell,
Lochiel, Nelson, Trenton, Fortunatus, Maxim, and
others I have seen, were all capable of holding their
own in any company.   Lochiel was a horse I very
much fancied, and over all distances he was a good
one.   Malua I might have named, and I certainly

must include Commotion as a wonderfully good horse. There were others before my time even better than some of these I have named.

Over six furlongs to a mile, I think, Fortunatus, under big weights, would have made any English flier I have seen gallop his best.

If it came to betting, and I had the requisite amount of cash handy, I would back such a horse as Strathmore was as a three-year-old to give Le Justicier, the winner of the last Eclipse Stakes, 10 lbs. and a beating.

Two of the best horses I ever saw in England were Isonomy and Barcaldine, and I think Peter, when he was in the humour, was about as good a horse as they make them. I never saw Ormonde or St. Simon race, so cannot say what they were from my own knowledge. Given as good a horse as Isonomy was the day Tom Cannon won the Manchester Cup on him, I should never want anything better.

What a race it would have been over two miles, 10st. each, between Carbine and Isonomy. It would not have been an easy snap for Mr. Gretton's horse as one gentleman fancied.

When we consider the number of racehorses in England compared with Australia, I think it may fairly be claimed that Colonial horses are an all-round good lot. There are in proportion more first-class racehorses in Australia than in England, I mean horses that are regarded as first-class. Of course, there are more good horses in England in point of numbers.

It would surprise a stranger from the old country, well versed in the management of horses, to see how some of the up country horses are ridden and driven. Most of the station horses are really wonderful, and how they stand the work is a mystery, as they are fed almost entirely on grass, when there is any.

Mr. E. Arnold, the manager of Winbar Station, Louth, in the west of New South Wales, has had great experience with horses. Winbar Station, I might add, is not a small place. It is one of the largest sheep runs in the Colony, and comprises an area of 960 square miles, or, in other words, 582,000 acres.

During the shearing season the mustering horses, that is, horses used by the men who muster the sheep, are changed fortnightly. So that for two weeks at a stretch they have to carry seldom less than 12st. day after day a distance of from forty to fifty miles, over stony country and broken ground, frequently stumbling into rabbit burrows, etc., and yet they stand it year after year. On Winbar Station they have horses eighteen and nineteen years old as clean on the legs as ever they were, and as sure-footed as anyone could wish. I need hardly say there is good blood in their veins, as most of them are the progeny of Coxcomb, who was by Yattendon. Horses have carried a 13st. man from Winbar to Bourke, a distance of nearly ninety miles, in a day of twelve hours. These horses have wonderful powers of endurance, and although not much to look at are very deceptive when tackled.

Occasionally these well-bred stallion horses are used as a "take down." I will give an illustration of what I mean.

A bushman calls at an inn in a small up country village. He is mounted on an animal with shaggy hair and a generally unkempt appearance — the sort of horse a London coster would be inclined to pit his donkey against. The bushman primes himself and those in the inn with liquor, and in the course of conversation it comes out that one of the company has a horse he fancies can race.

"My old horse can gallop a bit," says the bushman, at which there is a roar of laughter.

The bushman pretends to wax wroth, and after much argument he agrees to run his horse against the best any man has in the room for five or ten pounds aside.

The challenge is at once taken up, and when the shaggy-looking animal begins to race it is generally a case of the bushman's nag first and the local champion distanced.

The up country folk in Australia are the most

sporting community I know of, and they never lose a chance of making a match.

The buggy - horses are driven at a pace that would astonish anyone unaccustomed to the rapid mode of progression universally adopted. A dozen miles at a fair gallop is a mere trifle, and as a rule the driver returns home at a faster rate, and the dozen miles are covered in double quick time. For endurance and speed it would be a hard matter to beat these bush-bred horses.

In the large towns are to be seen some fine carriage-horses, but in this class the Colonies are naturally a long way behind England. There are some good carriage pairs, but they are few and far between, and only an occasional four-in-hand is to be met with.

In cobs, hacks, and carriage-horses there is great need for improvement. At some of the Shows fine turnouts are to be seen, but the majority of those met with every day on the road are not by any means first class.

Perhaps the best carriage-horses are to be seen in the cars of Messrs. Anthony Horden & Co., of Sydney, and Mr. Sam Horden is a big buyer in this line. There is not the care bestowed upon horses in Australia there ought to be, and many of them are sadly over-driven.

Heavy draught-horses are also much inferior to

those in the old country, although some farmers have a good stamp of horse, and the brewers' and contractors' drays are well horsed. The small tip-carts used would not be considered a fair load for a horse in England; in fact, I think a good English cart-horse would pull three times as much as an ordinary carter's horse in Australia. Hunters are not in very great demand, and although there are packs of drag hounds they are not particularly popular. Hunters, as a rule, are, I believe, better in New Zealand. At some of the Agricultural Shows, however, there are good displays of jumping, and at Bathurst, Albury, and Sydney I have seen some first class fencers.

There is too much reckless driving in the large cities, and the wonder is how people escape the dangers of the streets.

On Sunday afternoon the Randwick road to Coogee, a small watering-place about six miles from Sydney, is a sight worth seeing.

Hundreds of vehicles of all kinds are out, many of them sulkies with fast trotters in the shafts. These sulkies are driven at a great pace, and there is a desire on the part of each driver to get in front and head the procession.

A spill or two is not thought much of, and a buggy or sulky minus a wheel merely excites derision, and the unfortunate owner is mercilessly chaffed.

Pony-racing has obtained a great hold in Australia, to the detriment of horse-racing. This class of sport is all very well in its way, but it ought to be kept within reasonable bounds.

I have seen ponies running on racecourses round Sydney that could beat horses for speed over four or five furlongs. There are measurements for ponies and galloways, and they have to pass under the standard before they are eligible to run. I fancy the measurements are a bit mixed at times, as I have seen good big horses running as 14·2 and less. All sorts of dodges were at one time resorted to in order to get horses "under the bar," and so have them classed as galloways.

Paring a horse's hoofs is a common practice, and sometimes the poor brute suffered intense pain on account of the hoof being so cut down. A hot iron placed across the wither a few times caused the horse to shrink from the touch when the measuring bar was put on.

I have seen a horse measured at full stretch with his hind legs and fore legs as far out as he could get them. This made a considerable difference in his height.

Some of these measurements were obviously so unfair that an outcry was made about them and an improvement for the better effected. It was not the fault of the official measurer but of the men he worked for, who ran the courses and wished to get as many horses as possible under the standard. It was no uncommon thing when a horse had been tried and failed in ordinary races, to see it passed under the standard and figuring as a galloway or even a pony.

Pony-races are well attended, and provide good sport, and if the number of meetings of this class were restricted within measurable bounds there could be no objection to it.

Some of these racing ponies put up very smart performances, and a lot of money changes hands over the races.

There were hundreds of ponies racing in and around Sydney and Melbourne when I left, and I have seen over a hundred start at one afternoon meeting in half-a-dozen events.

India is a great market for Colonial horses of the better class, and also for racehorses and ponies. Some good racehorses have been sent to India to win the Viceroy's Cup for a rich Maharajah, and Myall King and Highborn were two of the best in my time. Sprig o' Myrtle is another good one sent over, and others I could name. "Teddy" Weekes was the principal buyer of racehorses for India before his death, and he was the terror of all owners of decent Selling Platers. "Teddy" made many a good deal in buying a horse out of a selling race. He was roundly abused at times for "bidding up," but he had an unlimited amount of self-confidence, which generally pulled him through and routed his opponent.

There is a tendency on the part of Australian owners to make the Indian buyers bleed freely when making purchases.

This is a mistake. A seller, of course, likes to get a good price for his horse, but he should bear in mind that even a rich Maharajah does not care to pay three times more than a horse is worth.

A much better price can be obtained for a race-horse to go to India than could be got for him in the Colonies. No one in the Colonies would have given half the price for either Highborn or Sprig o' Myrtle that was paid for them to go to India, because their form was fully exposed and their weight up.

India is too good a market for the Australian horsebreeder to play fast and loose with.

Every endeavour ought to be made to inspire buyers with confidence.

By all means get a good price for the horses sold to Indian sportsmen, but at the same time they should be treated so that they will readily purchase again.

A good Australian racehorse can be purchased, even at over his value, for much less than an

English racehorse of the same stamp, and the Indian buyer very often has the sense to know this.

The Viceroy's Cup is a much-coveted trophy, and an Indian sportsman can generally pick up a racehorse in Australia good enough to win it once, if not twice.

CHAPTER XI.

TRAINING AND RIDING.

On the track. Early training. Some gallops. Timing the
horses. Differences of opinion. Affable trainers. Tricks
of the trade. Notable jockeys. Tom Hales. His good
fortune. How they ride. Behind the scenes. An amusing
incident. Gallagher scores. The reason why. Steeplechase riders. Accidents. A Jockey's Club. Fees and
engagements.

It is not my intention to write about training as an
art, or about riding as a profession, but merely to
give an idea of the practice of both in the Colonies.
The Australian trainer does not differ materially from
his English confrere, nor does the Colonial jockey
differ much from the English rider; although both
adopt slightly different methods in attaining their end.

There is nothing more exhilarating than to take a
long walk in the early morning to the racecourse to
see the horses do their work. In Australia especially,
this part of day is the best, because the sun is
unpleasantly strong the greater portion of the day.
Many pleasant hours I have spent both at Randwick

and Flemington on the training track, when the dew
is on the grass and the sun's rays give quite enough
warmth to be pleasant.

The scene is Randwick, the time about five a.m.,
or perhaps before.

A rapid walk along the Randwick Road brings us
in sight of the famous course, and strings of thoroughbreds with their clothing on may be seen coming
towards the entrance gates to do their morning gallop.
How much depends upon those gallops only racing
men know. The various boxes are all occupied by
half-past five, some at the Lower Randwick side of
the course and others near the main entrance.

A few owners rattle up in their cabs, and the
trainers come along either in buggies or on horseback.

There is a fair sprinkling of spectators, who have
permission to be present, and also the representatives
of the sporting press, whose business it is to give an
account of the gallops in their various journals.

Reporting the work of horses is not looked upon
as a degrading profession in Australia, and the men
who chronicle the gallops are well up in their work,
and treat all with fairness.

Timing horses in their work is the rule, and when
the papers come out with the training notes in, the
times registered for a mile, or whatever the distance
of the gallop, are inserted.

I am not a great believer in the " watch " on the

track, although I do not think there is a trainer in
Australia who does not time his horses in an important
gallop. It is very different for a trainer, who knows
the exact weights the horses have up, to time a gallop,
to the ordinary looker-on who does not know the
weights.

Australian trainers place a great reliance on the
time test, and, judging by results, they appear to do
very well on it.

Certainly the watch tells whether a horse has done
a fast gallop or a slow one, and if every horse would
run up to his time in a race the test would be satisfactory.   Horses, however, do not always run up to
their trials either with a watch on or off.

There is a vast difference between a gallop on a
training track and in an actual race, the conditions
are so different.

In a trial a horse has a clear course and can do his
best; in a race he may be hampered by a big field, get
blocked on the rails, or the pace may not be fast
enough for him.

As the horses gallop round the Randwick track
they are eagerly watched, and it is surprising how
quickly the onlookers get to know the horses by name.

Some trainers make a practice of being early on
the track in order to have the ground in the best
possible condition before it has been galloped on. It
is often a race between Mr. W. Kelso and Mr. Harry

Giltinan who shall be first out, and Mr. E. Keys
generally disgusts the pressmen by delaying his work
until a late hour. It is amusing to a stranger unaccustomed to the sight to see perhaps fifty or sixty
people with stop-watches in their hands, all bent upon
taking the correct time.

When a pair of well-known fliers come on to the
track every eye is upon them, and an eager watch is
kept to see where they break away from.

Perhaps a trial takes place between horses in
different stables.

One trainer will say to another, "Give me a go
with Oxide this morning," and the answer is generally
a ready acquiescence.

Three horses come on to the track, for instance,
I will say Oxide, Chatham, and Newman. They canter
down to the mile post and then break into a gallop.

No sooner are they off than the watches are set
going, and at the end of five furlongs a look is taken
to see how fast they are going. On they come, and as
they pass the judge's box the watches are stopped and
the time for the mile taken.

Then it is amusing to hear the remarks passed.

"What do you make it," says one man with an
elaborate gold chronometer.

"Forty-seven," replies a man with a silver watch
the size of a Spanish onion, or less. He means
1 min. 47 sec.

"I made it forty-seven and a-half," is the reply.

"Then you're wrong. Here, what do you make it, Will?"

"Forty-seven and a tick."

"Ah, that's more like it."

Then the trainer of Chatham, who has won the trial, comes up, watch in hand, to a pressman.

"What did you make it?" he asks.

An answer is given, pretty fast time.

"I don't think it was as good as that," says the trainer doubtfully. "Don't you think it was nearer?" and he names a time.

Trainers do not care for particularly fast times to appear in the papers, but as a rule they are dealt fairly by in this respect, and if there is a difference of opinion the longer time is generally given. This is far more satisfactory, both to trainers and the public, for many men will back a horse on the strength of a very fast gallop recorded in the paper.

It will be seen that timeists, like other people, occasionally differ, and arguments are often heated over the correctness of a particular time.

Good-natured chaff is carried on at these morning gallops, and many of the men have nicknames, which are freely used.

Most of the trainers are genial men, and talk and spin yarns, and chat about the merits of horses in the most affable manner.

As a general rule a trainer will talk more freely about the doings of other trainers' horses than he will about his own.

In addition to keenly watching the trial of his own horses, the trainer will also keep anxious eyes on the gallops of other trainers' horses.

A comparison of the times made shows him which is the fastest go of the morning, and he draws his own deductions as to the merits of the gallop.

Ruses are resorted to at times to deceive or out-general the "clocker" on the look-out for a good gallop. A well-known pair of horses will be cantered and then suddenly break away from an unexpected part of the track, and the wily watcher, not anticipating this movement, misses the time.

I have known trainers gallop their horses before it was light, and even by moonlight, but I never knew any good come of these trials. One Victorian trainer was particularly fond of what the racing men call "sneaking a go," and he was up at all hours galloping his horses. He never, to my knowledge, brought off a coup.

Five o'clock in the summer and half-past six in the winter is early enough to gallop horses.

Randwick is a much better course for seeing the training than Flemington, as at the Victorian head-quarters horses are galloping on many different tracks at a considerable distance from each other.

At Randwick the course proper, that is the course on which the races are run, is thrown open about a fortnight before a big race meeting for the trainers to work their horses on, if it is in a condition to stand it, and there has not been too much rain. Hurdles are generally put out on the particular part the races are run on so that the gallops are generally wide. The bulk of the work is done on the tan track and the inner track, and there is a separate course for the jumping horses to be exercised over the hurdles.

The tracks at Flemington are somewhat similar to those at Randwick, but they are apt to become harder, and the Sydney trainers often grumble about them. Taken all round, both Randwick and Flemington are excellent training grounds, and their caretakers are men who look well after their work. The stables at both places are nearly all within easy distance of the courses. Australian trainers are hard workers, and look after their horses personally. They do not leave much to the "head lad," although he has authority when their duties call them away from home.

Personal supervision is what every trainer ought to give to his horses, and nothing should be left to chance. A trainer ought to be as well acquainted with the peculiarities of his horses and their temperament, both in and out of the stable, as he is with those of his children, if he has any. All the Australian trainers I have met are enthusiastic in their business, and spare neither time nor trouble in their endeavours to do justice to the horses in their charge.

Good jockeys are few and far between. Many men are able to ride a horse, but this does not constitute a good jockey. Race-riding is an art that few men, and hardly any boys, are proficient in. When I first went to Australia Tom Hales was at the height of his fame as a jockey, but of late years he has almost given up riding and is rarely seen in the saddle.

Tom Hales, in my humble opinion, is one of the best men I ever saw ride a racehorse. He has marvellous hands, a clear, cool head, is a wonderful judge of pace, a great finisher, and has a good seat. Above all, he is as honest as the day, and there has never been a whisper of suspicion against him during his long career in the saddle.

I have known Hales a long time, and his modest unassuming manner and thorough straightforwardness have always favourably impressed me.

Pleasant hours have I spent with him, both on the turf and off, more especially in his beautiful home, Acmeville, at Moonee Ponds, near Melbourne.

Acmeville is a charming bijou residence, furnished in excellent taste, and is luxurious without being ostentatious. Mrs. Hales is a model wife, and is a daughter of South Australia's most successful breeder of horses.

Tom Hales at home is a hospitable host, and

although not given to talk much he converses pleasantly on past victories in which he has ridden great horses. His record stands out alone, and he has ridden more winners than any other jockey in the Colonies. He has won nearly every race of importance on the Australian turf, and his classical wins are too numerous to mention.

As a rider of two-year-olds he may be placed on a par with that master of the art, Tom Cannon. Hales has a wonderful sympathy with the horse he rides, and he and his mount appear to understand each other thoroughly. In such races as the Derby, Hales' great judgment stands him in good stead, and his knowledge of pace was never better displayed than when he beat Carbine on Ensign in the Derby of 1888.

It was in this class of race for the late Hon. James White Hales scored his biggest wins, and he rode scores of winners for the Newmarket stable.

Unfortunately Tom Hales is a great sufferer from asthma and is anything but strong. His love of riding, however, is as keen as ever, and the last time I was at Acmeville he returned with me to Melbourne in order to go on that night to Caulfield to ride one of his own horses at work next morning.

"I never consider any trouble or inconvenience it may cause me," he said, when I asked him why he left his comfortable home to go out to Caulfield, "when there is work to be done. I have always made it a practice through life to be on the spot when I am wanted. I have done this for owners I have ridden for, now I am doing it for myself."

Tom Hales is a wealthy man, and has acquired his money in an honest manner, and has worked very hard for it, I am afraid to the detriment of his health.

He has a fine stud farm at Halesville, near Albury, in a lovely country near the banks of the Murray, and here he is devoting much of his time to the breeding of blood stock. He purchased Lochiel, the famous son of Prince Charlie, but was induced to part with him, and I think he has regretted the sale ever since.

Australian jockeys have a different style and appearance to. the English. Many of them have heavy moustaches, and Tom Hales sports a large one, which adds to his appearance.

They are, as a rule, neat in their dress, and their racing outfit is complete. It is the exception to see a slovenly jockey, and owners and trainers fight shy of riders who do not look after their appearance. If a jockey is neglectful of his looks it is a pretty sure sign he is not to be depended upon in other matters. At the present time there are some fine riders on the turf. Such men as John Fielder, W. Kelso, C. Parker, Ellis, H. & F. Fielder, M. Gallagher, the Delaneys, E. Huxley, J. Gains-

ford, Tom Nerricker, the Goughs, Cusdin, J. Brewer,
Moran, the Cooks, Durston, Luckman, Harris,
Dawes, E. Power, Lewis, Cripps, Redfearn Howie,
Fountain, Trainor, Quin, Robson, and when in the
saddle J. Hayes, are all thoroughly reliable riders.
Over the sticks the late Tom Corrigan and Martin
Bourke were bad to beat, while Cox, Brewer, Nolan,
Underwood, Whalley, Keighran, Hendricks, and
others ride exceedingly well.

Of the heavy weights John Fielder and W. Kelso
are in the front rank, and for his weight I think
C. Parker as good a jockey as there is in the
saddle. I have seen this young fellow ride some
grand finishes, and he has a big winning list.
Martin Gallagher is getting on in years, but his
hand has lost none of its cunning. A good yarn
is told about Martin.

At Rosehill he rode a certain horse, and he was
called upon to explain its running.

The chairman had a horse running in this particular race.

"You could have been much nearer the winner,"
said the chairman.

"Yes," said Martin; "but I could not have won."

"Why did you not ride your horse out?" asked
the chairman.

"I got jammed in," said Martin, with a smile.
"One horse kept me in all down the straight; in

fact, this horse was 'shepherding' me all through the race."

"And whose horse was that?" indignantly asked the chairman.

"Yours, sir," was the quiet but very effective reply.

Nothing came of that inquiry.

Jockeys are often accused of pulling horses when they are not in fault, but I am sorry to say I have seen horses deliberately "stopped."

In the majority of cases the men who instruct the jockeys how to ride races are to blame. If a jockey does not carry out the instructions he receives, he does not get many mounts.

An Australian jockey has not much chance of making a big fortune from riding fees alone; there are exceptions, but not many. An attempt was made by Mr. W. A. Long, one of the members of the A. J. C. Committee, to reduce the jockeys' fee for a losing mount to a pound. I wrote strongly at the time against this, and so did others, and eventually the fee was fixed at £2 instead of £3. For a winning mount on the flat a jockey receives £5. It is considerably more for hurdle and steeplechase riding.

When we consider the small number of mounts a jockey can get in a year, his income cannot be large. Thirty winning mounts is far above the average for a jockey in Australia in a season.

Jockeys are not allowed to bet, but they do bet, and heavily sometimes. It is a bad system, but it will never be avoided so long as a jockey cannot make a good income from riding fees alone. I have known of jockeys standing to win large stakes on races. They have told me the amount on several occasions.

It is a pernicious practice for an owner to put a jockey up and give him orders not to win, and yet this is done by men who ought to know better.

I once asked a popular jockey why he did not decline to ride a horse when he was given orders not to win.

"If I did I should never get another mount from him," he answered, naming a well-known owner. "Not only that, but he would influence other owners against me."

Another jockey was "sent up" for a time for riding what is called a "stiff 'un." This jockey said to me after the stewards had given their decision:

"I did not want to ride the horse at all. I knew if he didn't win I should be sent for. Mr. —— has had a dead set against me ever since I won on his horse at ——"

The particular win in question was on a horse that went out unbacked by the stable and simply romped in. It was utterly impossible for the jockey to lose on him.

On the other hand, I have known jockeys take an owner down.

I have in my possession now letters from a well-known owner of horses in which he asks my opinion about the running of a horse he backed in a race when he was not present.

From what he stated and what I myself knew I had no hesitation about giving him my opinion.

Accidents will happen during races, but many could be avoided if mere lads who know no more how to ride a race than they know how to fly, were not put up in the saddle.

These youngsters have no fear because they are unaware of the danger. There are far too many of these apprentices riding in the Colonies.

One of the worst accidents I saw was at Rand-wick, when Alec. Robinson was killed by Mr. D. Cooper's Silvermine falling. Poor Robinson was literally smashed all to pieces, and was hardly re-cognizable when brought into the casualty room.

In Grace Darling's Caulfield Cup there was a terrible accident, when Donald Nicholson was killed.

It is really wonderful how riders escape. Tom Corrigan and Martin Bourke were killed, one a few days after the other. Corrigan, about the best

steeplechase rider in the Colonies, was killed by
his horse Waiter falling in a steeplechase at Caulfield.   A public subscription was raised for his
widow, who got a good round sum.   The little
Irishman was one of the most jovial, good-hearted
men I ever met.

Martin Bourke was killed while schooling a horse
over hurdles at Flemington.   Bourke was a most
fearless rider, and the number of falls he had was
remarkable.   I think he had nearly every bone in
his body broken at one time or another.   Paddy
Nolan, another Irishman, is a fine hurdle and
steeplechase rider: this year he met with a severe
accident, and has taken out a trainer's licence;
and so is Harry Underwood.   J. E. Brewer rides
and trains his own horses, and has few equals in
the saddle.   He rode as an amateur for some time
before he joined the ranks of the professionals.

There are some fair amateur riders in Australia,
but not so many as one would expect in such a
country.   There are hundreds of splendid horsemen
in the Colonies, and yet very few men capable of
riding a decent race in the amateur ranks.

Jockeys have too much spare time on their
hands, and this is not a good thing for anyone.

I have repeatedly advocated the formation of
a jockeys' club-house at Randwick, or in the vicinity,
where the lads could pass away their spare hours.

In such a club they would be free from public-house surroundings, and would have their billiards in peace and quietness. Most jockeys, I find, are fond of a game at billiards.

It does not look well to see jockeys hanging about the entrance of Tattersalls' Club and other places.

Very few jockeys in Australia have retaining fees, and are constantly on the look out for chance mounts. For a big race-meeting a jockey will probably be engaged to ride for a stable, and certain jockeys may generally be depended upon to ride for certain owners or stables, but, as I said before, very few have retaining fees.

There is a vast difference in the way races are ridden in the Colonies to the old country.

Waiting tactics are not often resorted to, and it is generally a hot pace the full distance.

The severe two miles of the Melbourne Cup course is run at full speed, and there is not much chance of waiting on the road. This system of riding is in a great measure due to the time test. If a horse is timed to run two miles in say 3·29 or 3·30, then he has to do it in the race if possible. A slow run race is an exception. I mean, as a rule, the horses go at their top, but they may not be fast enough to make good time.

It would surprise many people to see the rate

at which horses go over hurdles and steeplechase fences. In a hurdle race the horses very often go as fast as they do on the flat. Steeplechases are often ridden at a breakneck pace, which says more for the pluck than the judgment of the riders.

In this chapter I may have omitted some good jockeys' names. Those I have mentioned are the men I am best acquainted with and have seen ride in many races.

CHAPTER XII.

SYDNEY is one of the most favoured cities in the world,
for it is surrounded with picturesque spots all easily
accessible and costing but little expense to reach. A
run of half an hour to one of the numerous bays in the
harbour lands one in a romantic retreat, far from the
busy haunts of men, and as quiet and peaceful as
though a journey of several hundred miles had been
taken. Yachtsmen may well be proud of the vast
harbour which nature seems to have made specially
for the benefit of lovers of the beautiful and for holiday
makers. On any fine Sunday hundreds of yachts may
be seen on the harbour darting to and fro like white-
winged gulls, sailing and tacking in all directions.

It is not, however, with Sydney Harbour I am
concerned. Its praises have been written by far

9

more eloquent pens, and its beauties described frequently and vividly. Many pleasant hours have I spent on that harbour, and felt all the better for the refreshing change after the heat and bustle of the city.

From Sydney to Liverpool is a shade under an hour's run in the train. On the Sydney side of Liverpool is the small hamlet of Cambramatta. Within a few minutes' drive of Cambramatta Station is Warwick Farm homestead and racecourse. It is a pleasant run from Sydney to Cambramatta when the orange trees are at their best, laden with a mass of bright coloured fruit contrasting vividly with the dark green leaves. After leaving the suburban stations the country becomes more open, and on either side of the line it is well cultivated. Cambramatta is not a very interesting spot, but when Warwick Farm is reached all is changed. The buggy is driven along a bush road, and an occasional glimpse can be seen through the trees of the stables and the Grand Stand on the course. The scent of wattle blossom fills the air, and the trees are covered with a mass of golden bloom. When the wattle is in full flower it is a beautiful sight, the delicate blossoms showering a yellow fall as we drive under the trees.

A large white gate, with a couple of huge wattle trees standing sentinel, is thrown open, and a short drive leads up to Warwick Farm homestead.

As the buggy pulls up Mr. W. Forrester steps out

and gives me a hearty greeting. The homestead is a comfortable snug spot and as clean as a new pin. Built on one flat, with a spacious verandah round it, it is an ideal summer residence, more in the style of a bungalow. Mr. Forrester is the best of hosts, a hearty good fellow.

We take a stroll through the spacious paddocks and look over the mares and foals, the yearlings and two-year-olds not yet put into regular work.

"Does stud farming pay?" I ask Mr. Forrester as I look round and see the large number of thoroughbreds that have not yet had a chance to earn their oats.

"I have had a lot of those mares given to me," was the reply, "and I have the use of a grand horse, free of cost, but I don't think there is much in it even then."

Honestly I do not think there is much in breeding thoroughbreds in the Colonies, for the simple reason the prices realized at the yearling sales are too small to prove remunerative. When an experienced man gives an answer such as Mr. Forrester did, it is sufficient to prove stud-farming is not a poor man's game.

In these spacious paddocks around Warwick Farm are some mares with the best possible blood in their veins. The lord of the harem is Niagara, a splendid specimen of a thoroughbred sire, and with much of the same blood as Trenton in his veins.

The young bloods are all quiet and docile, and they canter up to "the Squire" and put their noses into his pocket in search of dainties they often find there. The majority of them will stand to be stroked, and then at a wave of the hat they are sent off at a wild gallop round their domain. Old Noah Beal, the head man, is a regular patriarch, and must be considerably over seventy. He can spin yarns by the hour about old racing celebrities in the days when matches were all the go, and horses ran two or three heats in a day over a couple of miles. Noah Beal has been amongst horses all his life, and has trained and looked after some of the best.

From the paddocks we go on to the racecourse and walk round the track and see the horses cantering for afternoon exercise. The stable-yard opens on to the track, and there are a dozen or more horses in full work. There is Donizetti, the chestnut son of Marvellous, as fast as the wind, but a regular fraud. He turns up the white of his eyes and lashes out as I attempt to enter his box.

"You recollect the mile race he won at Randwick?" said Mr. Forrester.

"Rather," I replied, "when he beat Projectile."

"Well, I did not win a copper in bets over him. If I had not known too much I should have had a big win. They were flooded at Chipping Norton track (the Hon. W. A. Long's place adjoining the farm), and Mr. Long asked me if he could use our track. Of course I said yes. Donizetti had been well tried to win his race, and I thought I had a fair thing on. But when Mr. Long's Gerard did his go on our track it took the wind out of my sails altogether. It was a great spin, and I regarded Gerard as little short of a certainty. As you know, I backed Gerard, and my horse won. Gerard was left at the post. Such is luck. If there had been no flood and Gerard had not left his own place, I should have had a big win."

It was at Warwick Farm Highborn went forth to victory in some big races, and also to defeat in Carbine's Cup, already alluded to. Penance was quietly looking round his box as I went in, and near to him, Ronda, the second and third in Glenloth's Cup. Penance was a beautiful little horse, but a dire failure. With Ronda the Squire had bad luck, as he went wrong generally at the most critical times. It was always a pleasure to me to glance round Mr. Forrester's stables and farm.

After the inspection came a hearty meal, and the popping of corks denoted the champagne had been tapped. Then a chat and a smoke on the verandah.

"There were a terrible lot of wild cats about here at one time," said Mr. Forrester; "the beggars stole no end of young turkeys and chickens. I offered a pound a piece for their skins, and that soon cleared

them off.   Some of the youngsters tried to dodge me.
They occasionally brought in skins that had been sent
down from other places where a reward was not
placed on them."

We chatted over the prospects of the horses
winning in the future and of victories won in the past,
and when the time arrived to depart, Mr. Forrester
generally drove me to the station, and I was loth to
leave his hospitable quarters.

When I first paid a visit to the Hobartville Stud
at Richmond, N.S.W., the late Mr. Andrew Town was
the proprietor.   He was the beau ideal of a fine old
English gentleman, although a Colonial by birth.   He
was a fine, hale, hearty man then, with a cheery, jovial
face and a stout robust frame.   Bad luck and misfortune overtook him in later years, and when he had to
leave Hobartville, which had been in the family for
well nigh a century, it broke his health.   He gradually
faded away and died much as an exile would in some
foreign land.   It was like uprooting a sturdy old oak
to take Andrew Town from Hobartville.   It was a
thousand pities he was not allowed to remain there.
Hobartville is a splendid place.   The paddocks are
sown with English grass, and it grows luxuriantly.
There is an avenue of the finest oak trees I ever saw
in Australia here, and under their shade the annual
sale of yearlings used to be held by Mr. T. S. Clibborn,
the Secretary of the A. J. C.   The Hobartville sale was

a regular outing for sportsmen, and under the oaks
the most familiar faces on the turf could be seen,
much in the same way as they can round
Mr. Tattersall's rostrum at Newmarket. Some good
prices were realized eight or nine years ago, but since
the place changed hands the luck seems to have
gone, although many winners come out of Hobartville stud. Mr. Benson is still in charge as in
Mr. Town's day. The shady avenue of oaks was a
fine place to hold the sales. The auctioneer had his
rostrum fixed under a high oak tree, and seats were
scattered about in the shade for the company present.
The youngsters for sale were trotted up and down the
avenue, and they gave buyers a fine chance of seeing
them move. A splendid luncheon was served in a
spacious marquee, and the table was laden with the
best of everything, all provided from the farm. The
fruit was delicious, and the huge water-melons were
cooling and refreshing after the heat outside.

I have been at Hobartville when the bustle of the
sale ring was absent, and these visits were the most
enjoyable. In addition to the thoroughbreds, the late
Mr. Town bred some splendid trotting stock and also
draught-horses. Childe Harold was the trotting sire,
and a real beauty. Trenton, Grand Flaneur, Marvellous, and Far Niente were located there at different
times.

Then there was the extensive dairy farm, and at

one time over 250 cows were milked daily. Every
modern appliance in the shape of machinery was in
the dairy, and the bulk of the milk and butter was
sent to Sydney.

Mr. Town delighted to have a chat about pedigrees, etc., and his stud-book was very carefully
kept. When I looked over it with him I saw at once
the great care and accuracy that had been displayed.
Mr. Town resided in the town of Richmond and not in
the large house at Hobartville, and here he dispensed
hospitality with a lavish hand, and was always glad
to see a friend drop in at luncheon time.

There is a great change at Hobartville now. The
yearlings are inspected in the paddocks and sold on
the racecourse at Randwick. A special train conveys
intending buyers to see the stock, and during the
journey there is a luncheon laid out in the Pullman
cars. The trip is a pleasant one, and is looked
forward to by the trainers, owners, and others who are
invited to attend.

This is a chapter of jaunts and jots, so I will take
a run up the Blue Mountains and then drop down into
the City of the Plains, as Bathurst is called. It is a
six-hours' run in the train to the capital of the
Western district of New South Wales, and the line
runs through some romantic scenery. Before the
first zigzag was done away with a magnificent
view could be had above Penrith, over Emu Plains.

Coming from Bathurst to Sydney in the early morning when the sun was rising over this vast expanse of fertile plain, the scene was wonderfully beautiful. The train glided down the mountain side, and far away for miles beneath extended Emu Plains, with the Nepean river winding along like a silvery snake amidst the green grass and ploughed fields. The sun as it rose cast a glowing mantle of light and shade over this lovely view, and the colours were reflected in rainbow hues on land and water. Past Penrith, towards Bathurst, we came to the famous zigzag railway, which winds backwards and forwards up the mountain side to a height of thousands of feet above the sea. Leura, Katoomba, Wentworth, and Mount Victoria are all favourite resorts in the Blue Mountains, where the city folk are glad to go to get away from the heat of the town. Lovely scenery abounds in the Blue Mountains. Splendid waterfalls, wonderful caves, valleys, and mountains, huge rocks, and giant trees are all to be found as nature left them in the ages gone by. As the train winds its way along, a glance out of one window and you look downwards to an immense depth upon the top of trees and rocks; on the other side is a vast stretch of mountain and valley, all clothed in growth and extending as far as the eyes can see, until lost in the horizon. It is wonderfully beautiful, and so vast and awe-inspiring. Jenolan caves must be seen to be believed. No description would give an adequate idea of their beauty and of their extraordinary formation, and their mighty underground rivers.

We pass Lithgow, the colliery district of the mountains, and come to Bathurst. A charming city is the Cathedral City of the Plains. It is situate in the midst of a vast fertile plain, teeming with flocks and herds, and yielding the richest grain and crops. Many rich men reside here, and their vast estates surround the town on every side. The Stuarts of Mount Pleasant, the Lees of Holmlee, the Suttons, the Macphillameys, the Cousins, and the Sullivans, all have big interests here, as also have Mr. Gilmore and Mr. Rutherford. Tradition says that an ancestor of Mr. Stuart, in the olden days, when convicts ranged about in gangs, for his services to his country—he was an officer in the army—was told to ascend the highest eminence at Mount Pleasant and take possession of the land all round, as far as he could see. This he did, and the Stuart estate is an extensive one. This Stuart lies buried on the top of this eminence, and a monument is erected over his remains. I think the name Stuart is spelt correctly, but I will not be certain.

I was eighteen months in this district, and a charming place it is. Bishop Camidge rules over this diocese, a man universally respected. The Cathedral is a fine building, and the public park, on the site of the hideous old convict prison, is a credit to the city people. There is a fine hospital, a school of art, and a huge gaol. It is remarkable how these up country towns endeavour to get a gaol in their midst. The Court House at Bathurst is more commodious than the Supreme Court in Sydney. A lot of log-rolling is done by the country members of the Legislative Assembly in order to obtain big buildings in their particular districts. These public works ought to be called local buildings erected through the indefatigable endeavours of the member for the district, in order to bolster up his popularity. They have extensive railway workshops at Bathurst which are not half used, and they have a post and telegraph office large enough for a city ten times the size. The log-rolling powers of Bathurst members in days gone by must have been enormous.

Bathurst is a pleasant place to live in. The people there are hospitable, but there is the usual amount of side put on by a certain class of the community, noticeable in small towns.

Any amount of sport can be obtained in the district. Kangaroo hunting and shooting, hare drives, fishing at the forge, pigeon shooting, etc. The Macquarie river runs through the plains. Hundreds of hares are killed in these drives, and an ordinary visitor can purchase them for sixpence each, while a resident can get as many as he requires for nothing, provided he knows some of the driving party.

Kangaroos are numerous, and kangaroo-tail soup

is a luxury few people in England know the taste of. It is far before ox-tail soup, and is very strengthening. In Bathurst district so much is paid for scalps of hares, rabbits, etc., which are regarded as vermin. Many men live by killing animals whose scalps are paid for, and they make a good living out of it.

Many a good race have I seen on Bathurst course, and the Sydney trainers were fond of a run up the mountains a few years ago when the Bathurst Cup was a substantial prize. Picnic race clubs abound in the district at which amateur riders have the mounts. A ball generally follows the race meeting. Some of the gentlemen who run these picnic race clubs I have found out to be anything but amateurs when it comes to making a book—an amateur book, of course—or ringing in a good one to win a race. These "swells" are not above practising tricks known to less favoured and particular men on the turf.

CHAPTER XIII.

JAUNTS AND JOTTINGS—*(continued)*.

An Aldermanic jaunt. Lewis's Ponds. A breakfast lost. Electioneering. Establishing a newspaper. Legislators. A jaunt to Hobart. A glorious country. Brown's River. How we drove there. In Queensland. Brisbane sports. Old Vespasian. Scamp. A scene on the racecourse. James Tyson millionaire. His habits and character.

OLD residents of Bathurst have much to say about bushrangers, and how in days gone by these free rangers rode into the town and committed desperate acts with a bravado that would have astonished Baron Munchausen or the redoubtable Gulliver himself. For spinning yarns give me an old resident. It is a positive pleasure to listen to these gentlemen — they exaggerate with such unblushing effrontery. Some of these old inhabitants regretted the demolition of the ancient gaol as being the removal of a landmark that vouched for their veracity. Most of the roads about Bathurst are good, and were made by convict labour, and roads made in this manner are as lasting as the old York Road.

There are some roads I have been on which do not come under the designation of good, they are about as bad as they make them. Lewis's Ponds between Bathurst and Orange, not on the main road, very much off it, is a queer place to get at. I recollect on one occasion the noble Bathurst aldermen and the mayor, who was a friend of mine, chartered a four-in-hand coach with the laudable endeavour of forcing a road direct to Lewis's Ponds, and so diverting the trade from that then mining centre to Bathurst instead of Orange. I was one of the party. We had been invited to breakfast at Mr. Sullivan's at Rock Forest. We left Creasy's hotel brimful of hope. The mayor and aldermen were full of pride at the thought of exploring the route to Lewis's Ponds. I noticed our driver smiled grimly. He knew more about opening up comparatively unknown routes than we did. We rattled along pleasantly enough on a fair road, and Rock Forest loomed in view. It looked a fair homestead, and our stomachs after the drive in the keen air of the early morning longed to partake of Mr. Sullivan's hospitality. On we went until a creek was reached. We attempted to cross that creek. It was no go. We got as far as the centre, and had to get back as best we could. There was no breakfast to be got, that was very clear, and we could not reach Lewis's Ponds until after midday. We had missed the road to the homestead, and suffered in consequence. I shall never forget that ride. Never before were half-a-dozen aldermen and a mayor so jolted and jostled about. It was most undignified, to say the least of it. The coach had no springs—it bumped along at a savage pace. I made a request to be allowed to try the inside of the coach. I am sorry to say the request was granted, and we came to a halt. Inside was awful. At every extra strong bump I was jerked off the seat, my head came into violent contact with the top of the coach, and I was forced down again in the most off-hand manner. I was on the top of that coach again quickly, and got a seat between the mayor and the driver. When I was not holding on to the mayor he was holding on to me. Mile after mile we traversed. We were famished and holding on to the coach for bare life. The driver seemed to enjoy it. He had been bumped for the greater portion of his existence and was used to it. The question was, where did the road lie? I saw a track, nothing more, occasionally not even that. At one part of the journey we tore down a hill with ruts in a foot deep, and branches of trees had to be dodged in order to avoid losing what brains we possessed. Then we drove through a mass of thistles as high as the horses. We struggled into the village of Lewis's Ponds in a

woeful plight.   Our arrival was expected, but from
the demeanour of the inhabitants I should say we
were regarded as lunatics to have undertaken the
journey.   We devoured the entire contents of the
larder at one hotel and then searched round for
more.   Lewis's Ponds had been a prosperous mining
place, but it was gradually going off.   A meeting
was held to consider the advisability of opening up
communication direct with Bathurst.   Of course the
utmost enthusiasm prevailed, and also as a matter
of course nothing was done.   Opening up communication on such a road was out of the question.
We drove on to Orange, the road being a shade
better but not much.   The united thanks of the
party were tendered to the driver, but he hinted
he preferred whiskey.   We returned to Bathurst by
train.   How luxurious the cushions of the carriage
felt.   I met the mayor next day.   He looked de-
jected.   He said there was a Council Meeting that
night, and he felt he should be unable to take the
chair.   I made no inquiry as to the cause: the
reason was obvious.

Electioneering in the country districts of New
South Wales is amusing.   I have been in it and
know.   Freetraders during the period of strife hate
the very name of Protectionist, and *vice versa*.   A
local man is generally put up if one good enough
can be found.   If he has represented the town be-

fore, it is mentioned how much money he has caused the Government to waste on the place. The more money he has squeezed out of the Treasury the better his chance of success. The country, as a whole, can go to Jericho, the town is the principal thing. When the local Protectionists at Bathurst established a newspaper they roasted a bullock whole in the market-place and tapped barrels of beer. This was their way of showing appreciation of literature. The populace devoured the beef then; the butcher wraps the beef in the newly-established paper now.

On one occasion I went with a Minister of the Crown to his district in the Hume, near Albury. We went to Corowa, and he delivered a glowing speech. We feasted and made merry. But we had to drive in a buggy from Corowa to the Springs to catch the train, and it was a dark night. There was a fair road part of the way through Rutherglen, but we had several narrow shaves of being capsized over tree stumps and other minor hindrances to our progress. I have heard scores, nay, hundreds of election speeches in the Colonies, and every politician had a different reason for emptying the Treasury on behalf of the constituency whose favour he was wooing. Such an important question as the replacing of the town-hall clock would, he assured them, have his special attention if he got

10

into Parliament, and so on. If it was an agricultural district, the candidate promised the price of hay and corn should immediately be raised if he was elected. Politicians in most countries are humbugs : the Colonies are not blessed with politicians different from the ordinary run of such men.

It is reported of one gentleman, who held the position of Postmaster-General, that he invited his friends, ladies included, to oyster luncheons in his official room, and then calmly put down the expenses incurred in the petty cash account. I can quite believe it.

Members of Parliament have free passes on the railways and trams. It is a remarkable fact that Members of the New South Wales Legislative Assembly have always important business to transact in Melbourne about Cup time. This free pass business is a nuisance. Members ought only to be allowed a free pass when on a visit to the constituency they represent. These men have three hundred a year salary and free passes in all directions. It is a gross imposition. No wonder loans have to be negotiated. Members of Parliament are not alone in their anxiety to be in Melbourne at Cup time. The anxiety extends to the officers of the Australian squadron. The bulk of the men-of-war are ordered to Melbourne at Cup time. Strange the Victorian capital should stand in need of extra guarding at this particular period every year. I have gone rather out of my course, but crave the reader's pardon for the digression, which may not have been uninteresting.

A jaunt from Sydney to Hobart is very pleasant. Taking advantage of a favourable break in regular work, I took a run over to Hobart in the SS. "Oonah," of the Union Company's line, of which steamer the popular Captain Featherstone is in command. There is not a more manly fellow on the coast than "Bill" Featherstone, as he is generally styled, and he is a splendid seaman. Hobart is a curious old-fashioned place, built in the convict days; and Marcus Clarke, in the story "For the Term of his Natural Life," has given a vivid description of the horrors of convict life at Port Arthur and Hobart. The town is beautifully situated, nestling at the foot of Mount Wellington and facing the magnificent harbour which almost surpasses that of Sydney. Hobart has been described so many times that there is very little to relate about it that will be fresh to readers. This is not a guide-book, merely a slight sketch, or series of sketches, of what an ordinary individual's life is like in the Colonies. I often think books of travel are written for one section of the community only, the more favoured class of society.

During my stay in Hobart, I visited several of the training stables, and had a drive to the racecourse at Elwick.

The racecourse of the T. R. C. is prettily situated, and from the stand the silvery winding of the river Derwent can be traced as it flows on its placid way from New Norfolk. Some good race-horses have been bred in Tasmania, but sheep are the particular animals it is famous for. Some of the finest flocks in the world are to be found in Tasmania. Hundreds of guineas are paid for a good ram at the Annual Sales in Sydney and elsewhere. If I want to explore a town thoroughly I find it is a good plan to seek out a detective. In Hobart I was introduced to two members of the detective force, and one of them, Inspector Franklin, showed me round the curious parts of the city. There are some slums in Hobart, and the lower parts are decidedly not inviting. The Superintendent of Police, Mr. Frederick Pedder, is an entertaining gentleman, and many pleasant chats I had with him. There are some lovely drives around Hobart. The Huon Road is one vast panorama of superb scenes, and the orchards are an enchanting sight. I never saw such immense apples anywhere as in the Huon district. They are as large round as the crown of an ordinary sized hat, and luscious to taste. Tasmania is a veritable Garden of Eden. The inhabitants lead a very easy-going life. They appear to leave every-thing to nature, and she does very well for them. It amused me to hear that cattle were actually imported to Hobart from New South Wales to supply the butchers. Surely such a country as Tasmania could feed enough cattle to supply the people, but it would probably be too much trouble. Sheep are more easily farmed. For a man with a moderate income who wishes to retire from the busy scenes of life, I know of no better spot for him to select than Hobart or its environs. New Norfolk, for instance, is a charming country place, and situate in the midst of sylvan scenery. It has all the charm of an old world pastoral landscape with none of the disadvantages of climate. A more salubrious climate than that of Tasmania it would be difficult to find. At New Norfolk I put up at the Bush Inn, an old fashioned place, at that time kept by a sturdy Yorkshireman. The garden at the rear reaches down to the river, and it is full of all kinds of fruit, vegetables, and flowers. There is a huge mulberry tree in the centre of one of the grass plots, as large as a Sherwood Forest oak. Excellent fishing is to be had in the river. For newly-married couples it ought to be a magnificent camping ground.

A place of interest at Hobart is the Cascade Brewery, which is at the foot of Mount Wellington, and Cascade ale is justly famous. The head brewer, Mr. Todd, showed me over the place, and I was surprised at its dimensions. The water for brewing purposes comes direct from the mountain spring.

Brown's River is a favourite place for a day's outing. It is about a twelve-mile drive from Hobart. I was induced to undertake the drive by Mr. J. A. Murley, the purser of the "Oonah." Mr. Murley knew where we could obtain a useful sort of horse and a decent buggy. He undertook to deliver me safely there and back. It is no fault of his that I am alive to tell the tale. I shall always have fond recollections of Brown's River. It is, I must confess, a charming drive along the road, winding in and out amongst the hills which line the right hand side of the bay.

"There's something up with this horse," I suggested, when we had gone down a particularly steep hill.

"Nonsense," was the reply; "he's all right."

To prove the truth of the assertion, the horse declined to proceed.

I got out and examined him. Jammed in his near forefoot was a big three-cornered stone, which took some difficulty in extracting. No wonder he declined to move. He was not to be blamed.

At Brown's River we were hospitably entertained by a friend of my companion's. We remained there later than we ought to have done. Murley said there was a full moon, and I believed him. All the same the moon kept out of the way, and we had a nice drive home.

It was pitch dark. Murley said he knew the

road, every inch of it. I suggested it was not at all improbable we should have the opportunity of measuring several inches *on it* before we reached Hobart.

I am afraid it was a reckless drive. I shut my eyes and braced myself for the worst. A capsize into the harbour was the least mishap I expected.

We had no lights, and as we neared Hobart we thought it advisable to procure one, as the police were strict in this respect.

We drew up at a wayside inn with a wonderful sign, and obtained a bottle and a candle. The candle we inserted in the bottle after knocking the end out, lighted it, and I held it by the handle.

Candles have a habit of dripping. I rested the bottle-neck on my leg, and the grease made a beautiful series of landscapes on my garments. Driving through the streets of Hobart to the stables rude boys jeered at our beacon light and shied stones at it. Preferring to be run in to having my head smashed, I put out the light. No visitor to the Colonies should miss Hobart, it is well worth a visit.

In Queensland I have spent some happy days. I resided in Brisbane for over three years. When I went there in 1884 Brisbane was a flourishing place. Money flowed freely, and vast fortunes were being made by lucky mining speculators. During my stay there Mount Morgans boomed ahead on the market. I know men who made thousands in the course of a few weeks over these shares. One friend of mine cleared about fifty thousand. He lost it all and died a poor man in England not long ago. Another friend made half that sum : he lost the bulk of it at racing, but is, I am glad to say, getting it back on the Sydney Stock Exchange. They were stirring times in Brisbane then.

Captain Ricardo was Secretary of the Q. T. C. in 1884, and he was succeeded by Mr. J. H. G. Pountney, and Mr. Hyde, son of Mr. Hyde who manages at Kempton Park, is the Secretary at the present time. Eagle Farm, the headquarters of the Q. T. C., is a fine course and has a splendid stand. I have seen some grand races on this track, and the Brisbane Cup and Tattersalls' Cup were, in my time, good races.

With the bad times, however, racing has declined a good deal, and there are very few horses trained there now. Mr. Harry Walsh was one of the principal trainers, and a clever man at his work. Mr. McGill owned some good horses — Pirate, Lancer, and others; also Mr. Herbert Hunter and Mr. John Finney, J. P. Jost and others. I saw a famous old English racehorse in Brisbane. I went into McLenan's stable one morning and saw a couple of stallions in boxes.

"That's Darebin, the Sydney Cup winner," said the man in charge. "He's off to America, I believe."

"What is the other?" I asked

"That's an old English horse, called Vespasian," was the reply.

Yes, there he stood: gallant old Vespasian, whose victories at Goodwood were again brought back to memory when reading Custance's "Riding Recollections." Custance rode Vespasian in those memorable races.

At the time I saw him in Brisbane, Vespasian must have been over twenty years old. The next time I saw him was when he was led into the ring at the sale of Mr. W. H. Kent's stud at the Grange, Ipswich, near Brisbane. Poor old horse. He could hardly stand on his fore legs, and his hind legs were not much better. There was, however, a fiery look about his head, and he neighed proudly as he hobbled round the ring. He was sold for, I think, 120 guineas to the Bowmans, of Mount Brisbane.

I have seen some good stock of old Vespasian's running in Australia. Vespasia, a splendid mare, and Greygown, a real good horse, at one time being two of the best.

While writing of Vespasian I may as well allude to another good old horse that died in the Bathurst district of New South Wales, and this was Scamp,

once the property of the late Sir John Astley. Who
that saw it will ever forget that race Scamp won
at Croydon for Sir John, and which he so vividly
describes in his " Recollections."

Mr. W. H. Kent, who owned Vespasian, was,
and still is, an ardent lover of racing, and he has
during an extended career owned a lot of good
horses.

On racecourses in Australia the public are apt
to express their opinion freely when anything
suspicious takes place. I shall not forget in a
hurry a scene that occurred at Eagle Farm, Brisbane, I think in 1887. It was when Honest Ned
won the Cup. At that time Mr. C. Holmes
was starter to the Club. There were some hot
favourites in the race, such as Touchstone, who
had won the Moreton Handicap; Lord Headington,
winner of the Derby on the first day of the
meeting; Pirate, Theorist, and several others.
Honest Ned, owned by Mr. D'Arcy, was an outsider.
Some heavy double event books were then open
on the Moreton Handicap and Brisbane Cup, and
when Touchstone won the first-named race the
layers of odds had bad books on the Brisbane
Cup. At the start for the Cup there was a lot of
delay, and at last the horses got off to what
seemed a false start to the majority of the people.
Some of the horses ran the course, and of this lot

Honest Ned won. Several of the horses, including most of the heavily-backed ones, did not run but remained at the post. The jockeys on these horses declared—two of them personally to me—that the starter called them back. No notice was taken of the race won by Honest Ned, and the people were waiting for the horses to go back to the post and start again. To the amazement and indignation of the people a rumour quickly went round that it was a start, and Honest Ned had won. The stewards held an inquiry, and the race was given to Honest Ned the outsider. I have seen a few exhibitions of feeling on racecourses, but never one to equal that at Eagle Farm when this decision was given. The people rushed the Grand Stand enclosure and commenced to pull down the fencing. For a short time there was a riot, and some of the stewards were greatly perplexed as to what should be done.

The manager of the Totalisator took the precaution to retreat with the money to a safe distance until the storm was over. I never saw a racecourse crowd more determined to show how they felt about a race. It was a deplorable blunder on somebody's part, and it would have been better to have run the race over again, but as the starter stated it was a start, the stewards had no option, and awarded the race to Honest Ned.

I met Mr. Holmes the morning after as we were rowing across South Brisbane river in a ferry boat. He assured me he gave the word to go, and was very sorry such a start had taken place. I told him two jockeys who remained at the post said he did not say "Go," and that they heard him call out "Come back." To this the starter replied they made a mistake. It was a lucky race for the ringmen, as Honest Ned got them out of most of their double difficulties.

Brisbane is a pleasant place to live in, except during the very hot months. The whole Colony of Queensland has, however, suffered from great depression, and Brisbane itself has been fearfully damaged by floods. Nearly the whole of South Brisbane was washed away, and the huge bridge connecting the north with the south side was swept away. Thousands of pounds' damage has been done and many people ruined. I experienced one very severe flood there, when the rain came down in torrents for a week, and it was useless to try and keep dry. One hailstorm there I recollect well. The hailstones smashed hundreds of windows, and the galvanized iron roofs were riddled with holes. I saw, myself, the tops of buses perforated with these hailstones, and in my own garden we picked up stones twelve hours after the storm. The majority of these stones were the size of a cherry, and as hard as bullets, some were much larger.

On one occasion I went to Toowoomba, on the Darling Downs, to the Agricultural Show. There was a fine display of horses, cattle, and sheep, and some excellent jumping. The zigzag railway up the range to Toowoomba passes through magnificent scenery. This is the overland route to Sydney, Melbourne, and Adelaide. The train winds along the edge of the rocks, and a look out of the carriage window gives one a shock. The train is on the verge of a precipice, and a glance back will show that half the carriages are hidden from view by a curve in the line round the rocks. Vast stretches of forest are to be seen. The line is a triumph of engineering skill. The Darling Downs is a famous pastoral country, and there are some large stations there. The German settlers are generally most industrious and thrifty, and make excellent wine. They are very hospitable, and nothing pleases them better than for a visitor to call and sample the contents of their cellars. Queensland can boast of having the richest man in Australia, the millionaire, Mr. James Tyson. Many curious stories are related of James Tyson. He commenced life when a lad as a station hand, and by dint of hard work and thrift he worked his way upwards until at the present time he is richer than he is probably aware of. I believe, when the Queensland Government at one time were about to negotiate a loan, he offered to lend them half a million or so just to tide over any

little difficulties they might be in through shortness of
cash.   I have met James Tyson many times, both in
Sydney and different parts of Australia.   He is always
the same in manner and dress, no matter where he is
met.   I have seen him walking down George Street,
Sydney, from Redfern Station, carrying his belongings
rolled up in true bush fashion, with a slouch hat and
the usual old-fashioned clothes on.   He is a man considerably over six feet in height, thin, but powerful
and wiry, and his face is a true indication of the iron
will he possesses.   He is talked of as a mean man, but
I have heard of many unostentatious acts of charity he
has done.   If questioned about wealth he always says
if it gives his relations as much pleasure to spend it as
it has given him to make it, he will be satisfied.   He
lives in the plainest manner, a lonely life.   He is
seldom seen in company, and is a confirmed bachelor.
His one object in life is to make money, and as he has
wealth at his command this is easy enough to him.
When travelling by boat he generally goes in the
steerage, and is the sort of man who would ride
fourth class on a railway if carriages were provided.
One day when a stock-driver had ridden several
miles after James Tyson to tell him where some
horses he was searching for were, Tyson thanked
him and said, "Will you have a drink?" pulling a
bottle out of his pocket with a liquid in it the colour
of rum.

"Thanks," said the man, and took a pull at it. He spluttered it out, making a wry face.

"It's cold tea," he said.

"What else did you expect?" replied Tyson. "I never drink anything else."

I believe it is a fact that Tyson never drinks or smokes. Perhaps he has not time. Up to date Queensland also possesses the richest gold mine, or what was the richest in Australia, Mount Morgan. They will have a difficult task to beat it at Coolgardie.

CHAPTER XIV.

A COOLGARDIE PIONEER.

Ford, of Bayley's Reward. An interview with him. What he
thinks of Coolgardie. Nests of nuggets. Shovelling up
gold. How it feels to be rich. A salt lake. Three
hundred miles round. Betting v. Mining speculations.

MENTION of Coolgardie reminds me I know Mr.
John Ford, who, with Mr. Bayley, was one of the
first men on Coolgardie field and the discoverer of
Bayley's Reward claim. Mr. John Ford is a thorough
practical miner. He was on Croydon Diggings in
Queensland, and made several thousands there. This
money he spent or lost, and found himself in Melbourne minus cash. As Mr. Ford said to me: "Now
I have had the luck to make another pile I shall
not be such a fool again. It is not a nice sensation
when you come down to your last shilling."

His experiences on Coolgardie and the Murchison would fill a book and be very interesting reading.
It is a treat to see Ford smile when he gets hold
of a London paper with some glowing prospectus

about a Coolgardie mine in it. I fancy the share-holders would not have subscribed so freely could they have had a chat with him. I had two interviews with Mr. John Ford, which were published in a Sydney paper. The second of those interviews is, I think, worth alluding to in this chapter, more especially as gold mines in West Australia are attracting so much attention from speculators and capitalists.

If you are not rich yourself, the next best thing is to shake hands with a rich man.

A summons came to my office door in Sydney one day. Sounds ominous, but it was nothing connected with the legal profession. It was a knock on the door. A sort of knock that a man at once takes notice of. There are numerous kinds of knocks. I can always tell a hard-up, not-had-a-meal-to-day sort of knock. There is a timidity about it that is unmistakable. The particular knock in question was, however, of a different kind. It was a knock that plainly said, "I'm coming in whether you answer or not."

"Come in," I said, in a voice meant to be authoritative. A regular office-all-my-own sort of voice.

The door opened, and in came a gentleman I had the pleasure of interviewing once before in Melbourne, when he was unaware of my designs upon him. The result of that interview appeared

11

in print. It was with Ford, of Bayley and Ford, the pioneers of the famous Coolgardie goldfields.

It was Ford opened my office door, and when I saw him I fancied he might have come for his revenge for that interview.

"Well, how are you? Looking well, I must say : stouter than ever," said Ford.

"Who the deuce would have thought of seeing you here!" I said; "where on earth did you come from ?"

"Melbourne," was the answer. "Any objections to that ? "

"None," I replied. "Sit down. Not that chair, it's a bit rickety; take this."

I gave him my own. I wanted to have the pleasure of saying that a man who had picked up 200oz. nuggets had occupied my particular seat.

"What are you looking at ? " said Ford, as he sat down. "Do I look ill ? "

"Not a bit of it," I replied. "I was just glancing over you to see if there were any stray ounces of gold about your attire likely to drop off and lodge on the office floor."

He laughed. Ford has a jolly laugh. I fancy I could imitate it if I had had the luck to strike Bayley's Reward.

"What made you put that in the paper about me after I saw you at Cup time ? " said Ford.

It was coming. I knew it would. I was glad I had given him my chair to sit upon. I thought it might propitiate him.

"All right, was it not?" I asked.

"Oh, yes. But the beggars got hold of it in Melbourne, and when they knew who it was that was staying at ——, they came down in shoals. Had to clear out to get rid of them," said Ford.

I pacified him. Never mind how it was done. That is part of an interviewer's patent which must not be infringed.

I held out a few baits to my visitor, and soon had him launched on the golden topic, which is the mighty engine that moves this mammon-ridden world of ours.

"Ah, what did I tell you last year," said Ford. "Did I not tell you Coolgardie would turn out the richest goldfield the world has ever seen?"

"You did," I assented.

"Permanent, you ask. Of course it is. I never had a shadow of a doubt about it myself. I tell you, 'Verax,' Coolgardie is a mass of gold. The land reeks with it. The mines are extending in all directions. This new Londonderry mine is rich, but I do not think it will pan out as well as Bayley's in the long run. I know the country well, every inch of it, and that is my opinion. The finds are extending north-wards now, and it is in that direction there is the richest gold and also to the south of our mine. The main street there is now a mile long, and it is a populous township. Lord! you should have seen it when we first struck it."

" Didn't much like it, I reckon," I said.

" Like it! We could have hugged it. We did hug some of it. The first thing I hugged just before we got fairly on to Bayley's was a nest of nuggets," said Ford.

" A nest of nuggets!" I exclaimed. The fact took away my breath. Talk about the celebrated goose with the golden eggs—what had not Coolgardie laid for this man? It had laid the foundation of a big fortune, and it was hatched from a nest of nuggets.

" I saw one fellow peeping out of the ground," went on Ford. " I dug it out. There were three others followed. A nice little nest, eh? One weighed nearly 200oz., none less than 90oz."

" Here, hold on," I said, " this fact requires digesting."

" Digesting," said Ford. " I wish we had had something to digest at that time. We could not very well eat nuggets, or I believe some of them would have gone down."

" You had a hard battle to find the field?" I asked.

" We must have ridden 7,000 miles all told. It was a rough experience. The country is most extraordinary. Between Coolgardie and the Murchison there is a big salt lake which must be three hundred miles round. These salt lakes are numerous. Then there are masses of solid granite which rise out of the earth to a height of about 100ft. At the top of these is a hollow basin some 3ft. to 4ft. deep, and filled with water. I have often had a good bathe in them. There are curious-looking holes also in these rocks. The opening is about big enough to admit a small billy-can, but inside they are scooped out like a big oil-jar, and full of water. I have often got water from them by following up the trail made by rats, mice, and other small animals that go there to drink. The constant running in one direction makes a faint track to their holes. Their tracks can only be seen by an experienced hand. The blacks know them well, and can find these holes easily. It is an extraordinary country. It will, I think, in time, be a great country. As a goldfield I feel certain it will beat all ever found. In time I am almost sure it will be one vast goldfield from Coolgardie to the Murchison."

"There are a lot of men on the field now," I said.

"Thousands. But the majority are of the wrong sort. You meet the same class of men on all goldfields. They are men who have no experience, but follow on the track of a man who has. For instance, when a well-known man goes out prospecting these fellows dog round him. They camp where he camps, and give him no peace. They are as bad as the Chinamen, who never prospect for themselves at all. If I went out there prospecting again, I should have no chance. There would be a crowd after me in a moment," said Ford.

"Then you have no fear for the future of Coolgardie?"

"None in the least. I had thirty thousand shares in Bayley's, and have sold a few, but the bulk I hold."

"How does it feel to be rich?" I asked Ford.

"Not bad; more especially when you have been in Melbourne with a few bob in your pockets like I have," said Ford,

"How do you feel when you pick up a 200oz. nugget?" I asked.

"At first you feel inclined to shout. Next you are down on your knees looking if there are any more about. Do not think I exaggerate, but I can tell you when we first struck Bayley's you could almost shovel up gold. I never saw a sight like it in my life, and I have been on a good many fields."

When Ford rose to go I shook hands with him. I gripped him hard, in the hope that some of his luck might stick to me; also in the hope that some stray atoms of gold dust might be hanging on to

him. For a man who has made money as he has,
Ford is most unassuming, and there is none of that
purse-proud boasting I am sorry to say I have found
in a heap of men in Sydney with not half his ready
money. He is a man that fortune has not spoilt
but improved. A man I hope I may often meet
again.

This Coolgardie pioneer is as fond of a bit of
racing as any man I know, and he knows how to
enjoy the sport. Racing will never ruin him, because
he has learnt the safest rule of betting—that no horse
is ever worth entrusting with more than a fiver. I
asked him, as a man whose opinion was worth
having, which he thought a man was more likely
to have luck at, backing horses or striking a gold
mine.

He unhesitatingly said at backing horses.

I think he is right. I would sooner venture a
modest sum on the chances of a good horse than on
the chances of a gold mine turning out well, even
when it was struck.

CHAPTER XV.

THE most important racecourses in Australia are
Flemington, the headquarters of the V. R. C., and
Randwick, the headquarters of the A. J. C., in New
South Wales. Flemington is the most complete
racecourse I have seen. The course itself is not
better than Randwick, but the appointments are on
a more extensive scale. To see Flemington on a
Melbourne Cup day is a sight never to be forgotten.
Sneering allusions have been made in certain
quarters about the importance attached to Flemington and its Cup. It is noticeable that these criticisms
generally come from persons who have never seen
this sight. Even Max O'Rell had nothing but praise
to bestow upon Flemington, although his criticisms
of Australians are anything but fair, and his assertion

that England's possession of the Colonies was accomplished by the liberal use of whiskey, is too absurd to be considered seriously. Absinthe has conquered more Frenchmen than whiskey has Australians. Mr. H. Byron Moore is the secretary of the V. R. C., and he is the right man in the right place. Owing to his energy and unbounded resource, Flemington has become one of the most complete racecourses in the world; Mr. Moore has devoted years of labour to bring Flemington to perfection, and every year some change for the better is noticed. Thousands of pounds have been spent upon it, and the money has been well laid out. The lawn at Flemington far surpasses any I have seen in England, Ascot and Goodwood not excepted, and it is far in advance of those aristocratic club courses, Sandown and Kempton Park. The scenery at these places is as much superior to that surrounding Flemington as the latter's arrangements are to the courses named. If Flemington had such a magnificent view as Goodwood or Sandown, it would, indeed, be a racing paradise.

On all Colonial racecourses the public are well looked after and their comfort is studied in every way. Flemington possesses natural advantages for a racecourse. The lawn slopes down to the racing-track, and is beautifully laid out with flower-beds and fountains, and a spacious reserve for luncheons and

private picnic parties at the rear. The Grand Stand is
not high on account of the hill at the back, where
there is a cheap reserve for the people. There are
seats on the top of the Grand Stand, and at the back is
" the hill " upon which towers another large stand. The
hill is a favourite resort for the general public who
can sport half-a-crown for admission, and in itself
forms a natural grand stand from which the whole of
the course can be seen. Thousands of people can be
accommodated here, and all can see the races.

At the end of the lawn is the ring, and the
Stewards' and Members' Stand and weighing room.
Then comes Tattersalls' Stand, and it should be mentioned that at the other end of the lawn near the
luncheon ground and main entrance is the spacious
Maribrynong Stand. Close to Tattersalls' Stand and
the ring are extensive telegraph offices. The refreshment bars run along the far side of the ring near
the hill and under the large tower where the
scratchings are displayed is another refreshment bar.
This scratching board, which is an admirable thing for
giving information to the public, ought to be adopted
on every English racecourse. On this board are
placed the numbers of every horse on the card, correctly under each race. When a horse is scratched
his number is at once taken down from the scratching
board. The public can thus tell at a glance what
horses are scratched for any race as soon as they

arrive on the course. For instance, ten or more horses may have been struck out of the fourth, fifth, or sixth race before the first has been run. The numbers of these horses are taken down, which gives a backer every chance to reckon up the form of those left in. Thus in the majority of cases the public are aware how many horses will run in a race some time before the numbers and jockeys' names are hoisted. Such a plan would act admirably on English courses where so little time is given between the races, more especially when there is a delay of twenty minutes at the post.

Passing out of the ring the paddock is entered, and here the horses are saddled up. There is plenty of shade under the trees in the ring and paddock. Stalls run round the paddock, and there is ample room for trainers to attend to their horses.

Thousands of people go on to the flat free of cost and can see the races and enjoy themselves, thus having a cheap holiday.

And the cost of all this is a mere trifle compared with an English course with its scanty accommodation. The reserves on most old country courses would not hold half the people in the enclosure at Flemington on Cup day. For ten shillings admission can be had to the lawn Grand Stand and ring, and five shillings extra admits to the paddock. It is wonderfully cheap when compared with other racecourses. The half-crown

stand on the hill is better than the ten shilling stand
on the racecourse in England.   I am stating facts, and
any impartial racing man who has compared Colonial
courses with English will decide in favour of the
former as far as accommodation and reasonable charges
go.   At Randwick ten shillings covers everything,
including seeing the horses saddled.   The management both at Flemington and Randwick is as near
perfection as possible, and at Caulfield, the headquarters of the Victorian Amateur Turf Club, it is
the same.

Randwick is far more pleasantly situated than
Flemington, although it has not the lavish display of the Melbourne course.   Still Randwick
is a magnificent racecourse.   It is an easy drive
or even walk from the heart of the City,
and a ride of half-an-hour or less on the tram
The lawn is spacious and beautifully kept, and the
Grand Stand is a fine structure.   A splendid view
of the races can be had from all parts of the course.
Here, as at Flemington, the public are catered for
in every possible way.   The luncheon rooms are
spacious, and the carriage reserve is large enough
for the purpose.

The ringmen are at the back of the Members'
Stand, although they sometimes encroach on the
end of the lawn when a race is being run.   There
is a lot of betting on races during the running of

the horses.   I once saw a well-known backer and
owner lay a hundred pounds to one on a colt half
way down the straight with a lead of several lengths,
and then it was beaten and he lost his hundred.
The Members' Stand is a fine brick structure in
which is the weighing room, the Press room, the
telegraph offices, and at the far end the jockey's
room. The Press are invariably well provided for
on Colonial courses, and, as a rule, every facility is
afforded them for gaining information.

Space will not permit of an elaborate description
of these famous racecourses.   A very readable book
could be written about them and the many exciting
scenes that have taken place there.

I ought to mention that at Flemington there is
a straight six furlongs over which the Newmarket
Handicap, the Maribrynong Plate, the great two-year-
old race of the year, and other sprint races are run.
The Melbourne Cup horses start down this course
where they get a straight run, and then round the
bend, and cut into the straight course again in the
shape of a figure nine with a short tail.   At Randwick
there is no straight course, but it is a mile and three
furlongs round.

Every race finishes in the same place, in front
of the stands, and this is the universal custom in
Australia.   It is far preferable and much more
convenient than to be dodging about looking for the

winning post on courses where there are two judges'
boxes or more. The going on these courses is generally
good, despite the climate. English trainers cry
out at a spell of dry weather and lament that they
cannot gallop their horses. How is it Colonial
trainers can get their horses fit when the ground,
eight or nine months out of the twelve, is much
harder than in England, no matter how dry the
summer? Is it because the Colonial horses are
sounder on their legs, and have better constitutions
than English horses, or is it the system of training?
There must be some reason for it. Very few Colonial
horses are raced in plates, a still less number in
shoes, and yet the ground is often hard. One
reason horses can be trained so well in such a
climate is the care and attention bestowed on the
race tracks. Australian trainers grumble at the tracks
in their own country. I am afraid they would grumble
still more at many of the English tracks.

Mr. T. S. Clibborn, the Secretary of the
Australian Jockey Club, has had much to do
with making Randwick such a perfect course. He
is an energetic reliable secretary, but the A. J. C. are
more conservative in their notions than the V. R. C.
This is not Mr. Clibborn's fault, and I think if he
had a freer hand given him he would do even more
for Randwick than he has.

Caulfield racecourse is within easy driving dis-

tance of Melbourne, and is the headquarters of the
V. A. T. C. (Victorian Amateur Turf Club). The
arrangements at Caulfield are admirable, and the
lawn, paddock and reserves, are all carefully laid out.
The lawn at Caulfield hardly equals that at Flemington, but it approaches nearly to it, while the paddock
is spacious and well shaded with large trees. There
is ample space for the ringmen, and the Grand Stand
accommodates a large number of people. The course
is almost circular, but the home turn is sharp and
somewhat risky to get round in a big field.

To enumerate all the suburban courses I have
been on would fill many pages, as they are numerous.
I will allude to a few of the best.

In close proximity to Sydney is Rosehill racecourse, equal in many respects to Caulfield. Rosehill
is about half-an-hour's ride in the train from Sydney,
and the stand gates open on to the railway platform.
All the horse-stalls at Rosehill are numbered, and
trainers make application at the office for the number
of stalls required, and receive tickets with numbers
on, so that there is no confusion on the course. The
plan works well. The late Mr. G. B. Rowley was
Secretary when I first went to Rosehill. He was a
genial, popular man, and a splendid although somewhat expensive manager. He was unfortunately
killed by being thrown from his trap on the way
from the racecourse to Parramatta. The horse

bolted down a hill and upset the conveyance. Mr. P. O'Mara, who was with Mr. Rowley for some considerable time, was selected to take over the management, and, although a young man for such a position, he is well up in his work, and courteous and obliging. There is no more popular course near Sydney than Rosehill, and the Grand and Leger Stands are generally packed. Meetings are held there nine or ten times in the twelve months.

Next to Rosehill in importance is Warwick Farm, which I have already alluded to as the residence of Mr. W. Forrester. It is farther from Sydney than Rosehill, which is a disadvantage, but the meetings there are generally well attended. Mr. George Rowe is the Secretary, and he has been connected with racing for the greater part of his life. Mr Rowe is connected by marriage with Mr. E. de Mestre, who has owned racehorses for about half a century, and in his time has won many big events. He has also bred some good horses. Mr. Rowe is fond of a joke, and on the occasion of visits to the farm we could generally rely upon his affording us some fun.

Moorefield racecourse is owned by Mr. Peter Moore, and is at Kogarah, six miles from Sydney. It is a pretty little spot, and well managed by Mr. John Jolly, who at one time was in the A. J. C. office. Canterbury Park is another course similar in size to Moorefield, and the same distance from

Sydney. It is about a mile from Ashfield station on the main suburban line. A new line and station have recently been built closer to the course. Mr. Davis, one of the shareholders, is the manager, and he is another gentleman whose popularity is proverbial. Mr. Davis is always good for a day's outing, and if there is a picnic on he is bound to be in it. He is an enthusiastic fisherman and a very fair shot.

Hawkesbury Race Club held their meetings formerly on their course at Clarendon, near Windsor and Richmond. The H. R. C. is an old fashioned club, and the Hawkesbury Handicap, in years gone by, was one of the heaviest betting races of the year. The modern clubs have, however, given it a severe blow, but the meeting is very popular with old race goers. The Hawkesbury district is lovely, and orchards and orangeries abound there. From the course there is a lovely view in the direction of the Currajong range of mountains. The Clarendon course has been out of order for some time owing to heavy rains, etc., and the club held their last two or three meetings on Rosehill course. Mr. Guest is the Secretary, and has occupied the position for some years. Kensington racecourse adjoins Randwick, but is only used for pony-racing, although horses are trained there, and the going is generally good. It is under the same management as Rosehill. Rosebery Park, near Sydney, is the latest addition to the pony courses.

Round Melbourne there are several good courses, and within a mile or two of Mordialloc there are three splendid courses, Epsom, Aspendale, and Mentone. These courses compare favourably with the best I have seen, and good galloping ground is generally found on them. Their Grand Stands are elaborate, and all the surroundings of a first-class racecourse are to be found. As a rule the racing there is of a fair class. Sandown is another good course, but the most profitable is that owned by Mr. Cox at Moonee Valley. Its close proximity to Melbourne always ensures a large attendance. The Moonee Valley Cup, run the week before the Melbourne Derby, is a race that draws a large crowd.

Williamston racecourse is a bleak place on a windy day, as it is situated near the harbour, and is much exposed. Racing there is, however, generally enjoyable in the spring, and I have seen some capital sport there.

The general management of Australian racecourses leaves little to be desired. In several instances they show an improvement on the system generally adopted in England. The public are considered in every way, and racing is more of a pleasure than a business. Horse-racing ought to be

made attractive to the non-gambling portion of the
community, and it is endeavoured to accomplish this
on Australian racecourses. I have not been on a
racecourse in the Colonies where a good view of
every race could not be obtained. The races always
finish in full view of the people. There is an official
timekeeper for every meeting, and the time of each
race is posted under the numbers of the first three
horses. No one is allowed on the race-track between the intervals of racing—a vast improvement
on the English style, where people wander all over
the course. The clerk of the scales performs his
duties in the same manner as in England, and there
is no official stakeholder. In the Selling races
at suburban meetings the whole of the surplus
over the entered selling price of the horse goes
to the club, but Selling Platers do not fetch big
prices, as a rule. The A. J. C. divide the surplus
between the owner of the second horse and the club.

There is a decided inclination to abolish Selling
Races altogether, and this has been done at Rosehill
and almost entirely at Flemington and Randwick.
It will be a good thing for horse-racing when Selling
Races are abolished. They only foster discontent
and ill-feeling amongst owners, and are merely introduced into programmes to swell race-club funds.
Selling Races are responsible for many shady transactions that would, but for their existence, never

be carried on. They are merely gambling mediums, and have a deteriorating effect on the turf.

The number of short distance races is on the increase, but in proportion to the number run I think there are more races over a mile in length than in England. The Melbourne and Sydney Cups, the two principal races, are each two miles. The Caulfield Cup is a mile and a-half, as is also the A. J. C. Metropolitan Stakes, which was formerly two miles. Nearly all the most important races are run over a mile or a longer course. The chief race at the Suburban Saturday Meetings is always longer than a mile, generally a mile and a-quarter or three furlongs. The Champion Stakes, A. J. C. Plate, and Randwick Plate courses are three miles in length; the Australian Cup, two and a-quarter miles; the Cumberland Stakes and Loch Plate, two miles; A. J. C. Autumn Stakes, one and a-half miles; Canterbury Plate, two and a-half miles; A. J. C. Spring Stakes, one and a-half miles. Nearly all the w. f. a. races are a mile or more.

What surprises me in English racing is to see the vast number of horses stop when asked to gallop a mile. As a matter of fact, very few do gallop a mile. They commence slowly and finish fast if possible. It is no true test of a horse's merits to slow him down the first half mile of a mile race. An English jockey would be just as much at fault

in the Colonies as an Australian rider in the old
country. The two systems of race-riding are entirely
different. The Melbourne Cup, two miles, is ridden
from start to finish. This is not absurd, as I have
heard some English racing men say, it is the true
test of a horse's capabilities to get the distance.
Sprint racing is fast spoiling the staying powers of
the race-horse. Horses should be bred for speed,
but stamina should not be neglected. How many
two-mile races are run in England at the present
time ? There are not many horses can get two
miles. Not a fourth of the horses annually entered
in the Cesarewitch Stakes have the remotest chance
of running the distance out.

When starting machines were first tried on
Australian racecourses there was a considerable
amount of prejudice against them. The general
opinion was that the old system of starting was
the best, and the man with the flag would beat the
machine. To this view I inclined, but changed my
opinion when I saw how admirably the starting machine worked. It is mere old-fashioned prejudice that
stands in the way of its adoption all over the world.

In the space of twelve months the whole system
of starting in Australia was revolutionised. At the
present time the Victoria Racing Club and the
Australian Jockey Club are unanimous in favour of
the machine, and it has been adopted on the courses

at Flemington and Randwick. It is also used at
Caulfield and at nearly all the suburban meetings.
A great point in favour of it is that such starters
as Mr. George Watson and his son, Mr. Tom Watson,
think it is a vast improvement on the flag. Both
these gentlemen, the leading starters in the Colonies,
now use the machines to start horses.

Most of these starting machines are made on the
same principle. Gray's is very simple in its method
of working. A couple of posts, one each side the
track, with tapes across the track, and then by merely
pressing a lever the tapes and their supports fly up
away from the horses is the easiest way of describing
it. The barrier flies up rapidly, and there is no
danger attending it either to jockeys or horses.
These tapes comprised in the barrier are taut, and
do not flutter much even when a strong head wind
is blowing. The horses line up to the barrier without
the least trouble and stand like a regiment of cavalry.
When the barrier flies up they are all at a dead level,
and I have seen a score or more horses gallop off in an
unbroken line. Some horses are quicker on their feet
than others, and these get going sooner. Many trainers
now practise their horses at the machines, and it is
wonderful how quickly the animals take to it.
Owners of private tracks have had machines erected
on them to accustom the young ones to the flying
up of the barrier. There is very little noise attending

the raising of the barrier, not enough to frighten even a timid horse. Racing men who have never seen a starting machine at work will argue vigorously against it. They do not think it possible for a big field of spirited thoroughbred horses to stand quietly behind such an insignificant obstacle as the barrier presents. That it is possible I know full well, and no starter with the flag, no matter how good he may be, can get horses off as cleverly as the man at the machine.

Instead of long delays at the post, when a machine is used, the horses are sent off at the first attempt. Many a horse's chance has been ruined by long delays at the post. Constant breaks away take a lot out of a horse. Races in the Colonies are run punctually to the time on the card, and if the jockeys are not at the post in time they are fined. It would be an excellent plan to adopt here, as at most of the meetings I have been to since my return to England, punctuality is apparently the last thing to be considered. With regard to the objection that starting machines are dangerous, this I think can easily be dispelled. If a horse bolts, the machine can be raised quickly enough to give him a clear course. A horse will never bolt when standing up to the machine. He does the bolting in his preliminary canter, and then the machine is not lowered. A horse often bolts at the start with the man with the flag, but I never saw a horse attempt to bolt when lined up to the machine. Example goes a long way with horses, and if there is a horse disinclined to go up to the barrier, he soon gains confidence when he sees the other horses close to it. A fractious horse is more easily controlled at the post with a machine. Horses never rush into the barrier, at least I have never seen one do so, and I have seen hundreds of horses started with them. Occasionally a horse will snap at the tapes, but very seldom; and even if he does, no harm is done.

In his best days Mr. George Watson, the V. R. C. starter, wielded the flag as ably as the late Mr. Tom McGeorge, or Mr. Arthur Coventry. Mr. Watson has nothing but praise for the machine, and he starts with it at the principal meetings. His opinion ought to carry weight. The Americans, will, I think, adopt the machine in time. It is unfair to condemn the starting machine before it has been tried or even seen at work, as more than one English writer has done. If after a trial it is condemned, well and good, but give it a trial first. A satisfactory trial would, I think, lead to its adoption in England.

When I first saw the machine I thought it would be impossible to get two-year-olds early in the season to face the barrier. Much to my surprise the youngsters were got off with it at the first time of asking, to a perfect start, far superior to anything ever seen done with the flag.   Two-year-olds are not afraid of the barrier, and take to it kindly.

Every new invention has to meet opposition and prejudices. It is as well this should be so, for when the opposition has been overcome the effect is more lasting. In a new country where the people have new ideas, and are not imbued with antiquated notions, a startling invention generally has a fair chance given it.

CHAPTER XVI.

CRICKET AND OTHER NOTES.

Street scenes. Scenes at Sydney. Australia *v.* England. Some good players. Big scoring. An enthusiastic crowd. Johnny Briggs. Management. Scoring. A popular player. Football. Sculling. Yachting.

IF Australian horses have not had the chance of holding their own on English racecourses, Australian cricketers have had ample opportunities given them of displaying their powers on the cricket fields of the old country. That the Colonials have more than held their own when pitted against the best English Elevens, will be generally acknowledged. It is not my intention to write upon Cricket with the authority of an expert, but I can safely say no one enjoys a good cricket match more than the writer. Many pleasant days have I spent on the splendid Association Ground at Sydney when inter-Colonial matches and matches between England and Australia have taken place. The Australians are great lovers of cricket. The game has as much fascination for them as horse-racing, and their enthusiasm over a keenly-contested match is a treat to witness. A good match draws people from all parts of the Colonies, and at the final test match between Australia and England at Melbourne in March, 1895, thirty thousand people were present on the ground on one day. There were visitors on that memorable occasion from North Queensland, the wilds of West Australia, New Zealand and Tasmania, not to mention the adjacent Colonies of South Australia and New South Wales. Never on any previous occasion has there been such excitement over a match. It was the fifth test match, and each side had scored two victories. In Sydney the excitement was as keen as in Melbourne. Special wires were sent to the leading newspaper offices every few minutes and were posted in the windows. Immense crowds completely blocked the way in front of these offices, and many people remained there throughout the day anxiously watching the scoring board. The cheering was tremendous when an Australian's score gradually rose higher and higher, and when a fifty was placed opposite the batsman's name the thunder and applause was deafening. The crowd before the *Daily Telegraph* office in Fleet Street during the recent general election was not larger than that in front of the *Daily Telegraph* in King Street, Sydney, during the progress of this memorable match.

These enormous crowds are generally well behaved, and the police have but little difficulty in keeping order. To clear the streets would be a hopeless task, and very wisely it is not attempted to disperse the people. The excitement over this match rose to fever heat, but it is typical of the interest manifested in all important fixtures.

At Messrs. Lassetter's large establishment in George Street, Sydney, when a match is being played at the Association Ground, every run is notified by telephone specially laid on to the ground, and is posted on the scoring board. Throughout the day this board is an object of interest to some thousands of people whose business prevents them from attending the match. Every scrap of information is eagerly snapped up. The evening papers publish special editions with a couple of columns of description, and the complete score at the close of play.

On the cricket ground the scene is animated. The Association Ground, Sydney, is a model cricket ground. It is as perfect as any cricket ground in the world, and Ned Gregory, father of Sid Gregory, the well-known cricketer, is one of the best men at preparing a wicket it is possible to find. I think the members of the English Elevens who have visited Australia will bear me out in this. The ground, even in the driest summer, is a beautiful green, and the wicket, thanks to Gregory, hardly ever becomes worn, and in wet weather his pitches seldom cut up badly. The cricket ground is round. The members' pavilion faces it at the town end, and is a spacious handsome building, with a large gallery above the bar and luncheon room, and in front the seats slope down to the path leading to the ground on which so many famous cricketers have appeared. To the right is the ladies' enclosure. Beyond this is the Grand Stand reserve, with its magnificent stand and beautifully-kept lawn and promenade. A stand for smokers has been erected at the far end. Round the other half of the ground is the shilling enclosure, which is on a slope, so that no matter how many people are packed in it all can see. From any part of the ground a good view of the match can be obtained. No ungainly coaches block the view, and no carriages are allowed on the ground. The members of the Association wish every one present to have a good view, and the committee see they get it. This is as it should be. In the old country there is far too much catering for the privileged few at the expense of the many. The Australians would never stand such absurd arrangements as are in force at an Oxford and Cambridge or an Eton and Harrow match. They pay about half the price to see a good match, and obtain twice as much consideration from the management. It is a pleasure to watch a match on the Association Ground, Sydney. It is anything but a pleasure to do so on many English cricket grounds.

It is amusing to hear the remarks passed during the course of an Australia *v.* England match. A Lancashire and a Yorkshire man, I once saw nearly came to blows over the respective merits of the members of those counties who were in the team. It is not only the Colonial or the English element that waxes hot during these matches, but the natives of the various counties from which the players hail, and who have made their homes in Australia, argue strongly in favour of their counties' representatives.

Chaffing the players was freely indulged in some years ago, but there is very little of it now. George Giffen occasionally comes in for a share when he bowls throughout for his Colony against New South Wales. "Let somebody else have a try, George;" "Give Walter a chance;" "Sit down and have a rest, George." These are the expressions shouted out to the great cricketer, the "W. G." of Australia. In the last match I saw between New South Wales and South Australia on this ground, the former scored a remarkable victory. Garratt was captain of the home team, and in the first innings of the South Australians he fielded badly. He did much better in the second, but whenever he fielded the simplest ball, there was an ironical round of applause. It was the same with Moses, who was not in his best form.

In this match it looked any odds on South Australia, but the New South Wales bowlers fairly paralysed the South Australian batsmen, and they were all out, on the last day, before luncheon. Not many people were present, as it was generally considered the visitors would quickly knock up the runs required. I was, luckily, there, and a more exciting bit of cricket I have seldom seen. There had been rain during the night, and this may have helped the bowlers a little, but both McKibbin and Charlie Turner were in great form. George Giffen acknowledged that the bowling was good enough to beat any batsmen.

On this ground I have seen the only W. G. Grace score, but he was generally unlucky here. W. G. Grace is by no means the popular idol in Australia he is in England, and it would be long odds on Stoddart for the " Favourite Stakes " on that side of the globe. No more popular cricketer ever captained an English Eleven in Australia than A. E. Stoddart. He is a gentleman, every inch of him. It did one good to hear the ringing cheers that always greeted the famous Middlesex bat when he walked quietly to the wicket. The 1895 English Eleven was one of the most popular that ever visited Australia, and for this, in a great measure, the members have to thank their captain. A. E. Stoddart stands no nonsense in his team. He is a strict disciplinarian, and yet he knows where to draw the line, so that the tour may prove enjoyable. He strains every nerve to win matches, and works harder than any man in the team.

Another very popular English cricketer is Johnny Briggs, as he is always called. Briggs knows his audience. J. B. is the funny man of the team in the field. He is never still. He seems built on wires, and if he is tired he never shows it. Many a roar of laughter has Briggs caused through pretending to misfield a ball, and then, when the unsuspecting batsman starts to run, he picks the ball up as quick as lightning from between his feet, and shoots it in to the wicket-keeper with unerring aim. No one ever begrudges Briggs making a score. The Lancashire man and Sid Gregory, of New South Wales, are about equal for smartness in the field. I think, if there be a balance it is in favour of Gregory, who is the cleanest, quickest field, I think, I ever saw, and he is a remarkable bat. To see Gregory and Graham steal runs is a treat. In one match against Stoddart's Eleven, when both made large scores, they must have stolen many runs. I remember they roused the vast crowd almost to a state of frenzy, by the way they lashed the best bowling England could produce.

Two fine young cricketers I saw play were Albert Trott, the elder Trott's brother, and Clem. Hill, of Adelaide. These young fellows ought to find a place in any Australian Eleven before long. Frank Iredale is another cricketer who is sure to come over to England. He is a safe bat and a good field. I have seen him play some splendid innings. I have mentioned Sid Gregory, and for his size he is one of the best batsmen now playing. He can safely be placed on a par with Abel. No greater compliment could be paid him.

Donnan is another promising cricketer, also Dwyer and Darling. None of them have yet appeared in England. Like C. Hill, Dwyer and Darling hail from Adelaide, Donnan from New South Wales. Hill, I ought to mention, in addition to being a remarkably fine bat, is a very good wicket-keeper. In his best form Charles Turner was one of the finest bowlers in Australia. In my opinion he could always give Ferris a long start. I think the omission of Turner in the last Australian team against England in Melbourne was a mistake. Lyons was selected in preference, and, although, he made a good score in the first innings, Turner's bowling was sadly missed when the Englishmen were piling up their score in their second innings. Turner can bowl for any length of time. He is always a good man to put on for a change, as he can keep down runs even when they have been coming freely. McKibbin, a new bowler, created quite a sensation last season (1894–95), and, like Turner, he hails from Bathurst. He has a peculiar knack of pitching his ball, and George Giffen said there was

13

a certain ball which McKibbin sometimes pitched that no batsman could play. If he could always manage this particular ball when wanted, he would indeed be a wonder. Callaway at one time I fancied would develop into a fine all-round cricketer. He was a good steady bat, and a capital bowler. He, however, put on flesh rapidly, and in later matches did not show so well as his early promise indicated. Eady, of Tasmania, is another bat that has come into prominence of late, and there are many others I could mention.

The last time I met long George Bonner was in Orange, his native place, where he was leading an easy life. I can remember the sensational hits Bonner made when he was in the Australian team, eleven or twelve years age. The best Australian Eleven I ever saw in England was that captained by Murdoch in the early eighties. It was a remarkably powerful team, and gave the English cricketers a surprise. What a demon Spofforth was, and how his balls were sent in like a shot from a cannon. I recollect at Trent Bridge Ground, Nottingham, a young fellow remarked as Spofforth went back to take a longer run than usual, " He's off to the 'Flying Horse' for lunch." There were flying bails with that particular ball. The Bannermans I have seen play on both sides of the world, and also Garratt, Sam Jones, Bruce, Blackham, Massey, and many more good men. Bannerman generally umpires for New South Wales, and his decisions are hardly ever questioned. Blackham I am afraid will not play much longer, as his hands have been knocked about terribly.

Australian cricketers are likely to hold their own in years to come. The many parks and recreation grounds in the large cities afford the youngsters every opportunity to indulge in cricket. At Moore Park, Sydney, on Saturday afternoon, cricket matches may be seen played all over the ground. These wickets are reserved for certain clubs, and the matting is nearly always used between the wickets.

Cricket matches are well managed in the Colonies. The scoring-board is placed in a conspicuous position. Every run is recorded to the batsmen as it is got, and every change of bowling is put up. The total is added to with every run obtained, and also the total score at the fall of the last wicket. Thus the spectators can see at a glance how many each batsman at the wicket has scored, what the total is, and how many wickets are to fall. This system of scoring adds greatly to the interest in a match. As soon as the batsman's score changes from 48 to 50 there is a deafening cheer, and when it reaches 100 the scene is exciting. I shall never forget when Sid Gregory piled up over 200 against the Englishmen on the Association Ground, Sydney.

When the score went up opposite his name people cheered until they were hoarse. They stood on forms and frantically waved hats, umbrellas, or pockethandkerchiefs, and it was some minutes before the enthusiasm waned. For a hearty appreciation of good cricket an Australian crowd is bad to beat. I have merely dotted down these cricket fragments as they occurred to me while writing, and I hope they have not been tedious.

Football, too, has a great hold upon the public, more especially in Melbourne, where the game is played under Victorian rules, a kind of cross between Rugby and Association. It is no uncommon thing on a Saturday afternoon in Melbourne, when the famous clubs meet in the Cup Tie, to see from 25,000 to 30,000 spectators present. Considering the population, as compared with some great English cities, this is, I think, a most extraordinary attendance. A crowd of 10,000 people at an ordinary match, either at cricket or football, is an every day affair. In Sydney, Rugby and Association are both played, and the former is more popular, especially with the spectators. New Zealand is the place for champion Rugby players, but in New South Wales the game has improved wonderfully during the last five years. The English football team had, however, a much easier task set them than the cricketers.

Australia can lay claim to have produced some of

the best scullers in the world, and Beach, Stansbury, Matterson, Searle, Laycock, Rush, and Trickett stand out from others that might be named. I have often seen burly Bill Beach in Sydney. Unlike most athletes he has stuck to his money and not squandered it.

The last time I saw Trickett he was preaching to a crowd near the post-office, Sydney, much in the fashion adopted by an ardent follower of General Booth. Trickett is evidently anxious to scull towards the Golden Shore now he has given up dispensing liquor in a Queensland hotel.

Rush, when I left Sydney, kept an hotel at the corner of King Street and York Street; Beach's hotel, as it is still called, being at the corner of King Street and Pitt Street. Johnny Deeble, as he is styled, formerly kept the "Angel" in Pitt Street, now run by the genial Frank Wilson. Deeble makes a book and has given up dabbling in rowing matters. The Punches are well known in connection with sculling, and Frank Punch keeps the hotel bearing his name in Market Street.

One sculler has taken to bicycling and makes a very good show at it. Poor Searle's funeral in Sydney was one of the most impressive sights ever seen there. It gave the late Governor Duff's funeral procession the go by.

Many a time have I passed the monument erected to Searle on the Parramatta river, one of the best

rivers I ever was on for a sculling race. At Ryde
and Gladesville, where the headquarters of the
scullers are, I have spent pleasant days, and watched
Hanlan dash along in his customary brilliant style,
and seen Beach and the other good scullers pull on
this fine stretch of water.

Over one match there is a tale related about
certain newspaper men told off to do the account
of the race. Great rivalry existed between the two
evening papers, each of which had made every
arrangement possible to get the result out before
the other. The newly-started paper must have
risked it, as the winner's name was shouted a minute
or so after the race. Luckily it turned out to be
correct. The managing director of the opposition
paper was so wroth at being second in the field
that he stood at the top of the stairs leading to
the reporters' room and "sacked" each unfortunate
man told off to assist in recording the race, as he
came up the office stairs.

The Nepean river is not so good as the Parramatta, but some great races have been rowed there.
A considerable amount of interest is taken every
year in the international rowing contests. In Sydney
there are numerous rowing and sailing clubs, and the
harbour is alive with yachts every Saturday afternoon
and all Sunday. The sight from the Botanical Gardens
on a fine summer's day is charming.

CHAPTER XVII.

In the palmy days of the ring there were some exciting boxing encounters in the Colonies. Of late years, however, the pugilists have not had a very lively time, and when I left, the matches arranged were few and far between. The Sydney Amateur Gymnastic Club, when in full swing, was an admirable institution, and Mr. Corbett had the management of it. He worked the club up, and no fault could be found with the class of entertainments provided. All the principal boxing-matches at one time took place at this club, but ten years ago Larry Foley's Saloon at the " White Horse " in George Street, was the head centre in this line of sport. Peter Jackson is the best boxer Australia has produced for many years, and he

is what may be termed, in Colonial parlance, " a
white man," although his skin is black.   Jackson is a
quiet unassuming man, and in all his encounters he
has always behaved himself fairly and honestly.   He
never got into rows, nor did he boast of his strength
and pugilistic skill as several of the fraternity are too
apt to do.

Slavin, Goddard, Dawson, Power, Burge, Griffiths
" Griffo," Dooley, Jack Fuller, Ryan, Billy Murphy,
Foley, Bourke, and others I have at different times
seen in and out of the ring.   Larry Foley in his
prime was a man hard to beat, and he still retains
a good deal of his skill with his fists.   Larry Foley
is a shrewd man of business, and although he has
not taken his degree at a University he can hold his
own with men who have had more educational advantages.   He is fond of a joke, and has a ready Irish wit
that stands him in good stead.   He is, I should say,
well off, and with a credit of several thousands at his
bankers.   " Griffo " was the cleverest light weight
with his fists I ever saw, and Murphy was never a
match for him.   " Griffo " was, however, not the sort
of young fellow to get on in the world.   He was too
fond of his glass, and led a gay, fast life.   It was
wonderful how quickly he could get into condition
and was ready to fight with half the amount of
training an ordinary boxer would have.   When
stripped he was a perfect model—a regular pocket

Hercules. He was very game and never knew what it was to be beaten. The slavish admirers who surrounded him led him astray, and when he won money he spent it like water. He went to America, and the latest news of him there was that he " still carried on the same old game." Joe Goddard was a huge fellow, with a fist like a sledge hammer, but he was not a scientific boxer. He relied on his strength, and generally tried to rush his opponent and get in a swinging blow, so that he could not come up to time. Mic Dooley, as tall a man as Goddard, was very different. To hear Dooley talk one would imagine he was too mild to hurt a fly. A genial good-natured fellow, who through over generosity never could hold his own with the sharper unscrupulous men surrounding him. In "Nemo," the well-known writer, Dooley had a firm friend, although on one occasion they had a quarrel that might have ended seriously. They were, however, better friends than ever when they had cooled down.

At the time I was connected with the Sydney *Referee* we had a boxing gentleman, named Alfred Hales, on the paper. He had a style of writing peculiarly his own, and it took immensely with the boxing fraternity. Mr. Hales was a smart man, a real good journalist spoilt through want of early training on the Press. He could write upon any subject, and was never at a loss for humorous sayings. Under

"Smiler" he wrote some first-class articles. When
General Booth visited Australia "Smiler" was turned
on to report his arrival in Sydney on the Saturday
for the next day's *Sunday Times*. Judge of my
amazement when I saw "Smiler," the pugilistic
writer, seated on the box seat of the General's
carriage, and looking as big a "blood and fire" man
as any of the S. A. men in the procession. From
his own account he created a favourable impression
on the General, who was fully convinced "Smiler"
must at least be a captain in the S. A. Army. I
fancy Mr. Hales would have had to vacate his seat
on the General's carriage had it been known to the
occupant that he was the boxing scribe of a sporting
paper.

"Don't see anything incongruous about it," said
Mr. Hales to me. "We're both fighting men, Booth
and myself. There is only a difference in our
method."

Mr. Hales ran for East Macquarie constituency at
one general election against the two old members,
Mr. Sydney Smith, Minister for Mines, and Mr. James
Tonkin. Considering he was quite a new man, had no
money, like most journalists, and no influence, he
polled remarkably well, and had he kept up his
connection with the constituency, would probably
have been elected at some future time. He informed
me that the payment of a Member of Parliament, £300

a year, was not a thing to bo sneezed at. Mr. Hales, I remember, pasted up the occasional blue official papers he received in his office, and was rather proud of the collection. He went to America with the proverbial farthing in his pocket, and managed to travel through that country and England before returning to Australia. The last I heard of him was that he had started a paper at Coolgardie, West Australia, and that he had nearly been starved to death in the bush when exploring. He was a remarkable man, and never at a loss for something to do or say.

Mr. Ted Belisario was a great supporter of boxing, and also Mr. George Hill. Both spent a lot of money on the sport, and Mr. Belisario generally had his hand in his pocket when assistance was required. Mr. Corbett, however, I think, did as much to keep the sport legitimate as any man in Sydney.

When John L. Sullivan came to Sydney he was under an engagement with the Messrs. MacMahon to play in a piece written for him, called, " Honest Hearts and Willing Hands." Her Majesty's theatre was taken for the pugilist's debut in Sydney. John L. Sullivan was a dire frost as an actor. Probably the want of appreciation shown him on the stage made him eager to display his prowess off the stage. As the Americans would put it, he "went on a jag." Sullivan cleared bars and smashed things generally, and altogether quite upheld his American reputation in this respect. He was given a hearty reception on his arrival at the Gymnastic Club in York Street, and if he had been contented with sparring exhibitions he would have made money.

At these boxing-matches there were present eminent lawyers, members of both houses of the legislature, and prominent men in various professions and businesses. When the police commenced to take notice of these affairs, boxing soon went down hill, and at the present time it is at a low ebb.

When the Carrington running grounds were opened in Bourke Street, Sydney, there was an extraordinary amount of interest taken in foot racing. The Sir Joseph Banks' grounds at Botany, almost on the shores of the historic bay, had been established some years by Mr. Frank Smith. Big stakes were given to be run for, as much as £600 for a handicap or more. Thousands of pounds changed hands over these handicaps, and well-known bookmakers kept stables of runners instead of race-horses. "Backing talking horses," is, however, a risky game, and so it proved in the long run. We had several good runners in the *Referee* office on the composing staff. One of them, Charles Merchant, won the first Carrington Handicap, value over £600, I think, and in all he landed four of these handicaps. He must have won a heap of money, but I am afraid he has not kept it.

Merchant was a clever runner. He never knew what it was to be nervous on the mark, and that gave him a great advantage. There were hundreds of good runners then, and many of them lived on the game. Such men as Samuels are not often found on a running track. Charlie Samuels, as I have stated in a former chapter, was an aboriginal hailing from Queensland. He was a splendid runner, and in his matches with Hutchins showed what he could do. Hutchins, however, I do not think, was seen at his best in the Colonies. He was never properly fit, and indulged too freely. Samuels could run from 75 yards up to 440 yards as well as any man I ever saw. Thousands of pounds must have been won over him by Lees and others at one time or another, and yet Lees died a few years ago a broken man. Mr. Tom Rose, Mr. H. Oxenham's head manager, can spin yarns by the hour about pedestrianism and the tricks runners were up to. A well-known former English champion, Mr. Frank Hewitt, is in Sydney, and he can run now faster than many younger men. Mr. H. Rolston, a colleague of mine on the press, has had a good deal of experience with foot runners, and some articles he wrote were widely read and much talked about.

On one occasion I went with Charles Merchant to Botany Grounds to see the American Myers run for a handicap. We fancied he would win, but, alas he went down in his second heat and visions of wealth vanished. I saw Myers put up a quarter mile record on Sir Joseph Banks' grounds, and as he had to run round a big field it was a great performance.

Some excitement was caused after one Carrington Handicap. It was on Saturday night, the heats and finals being run by electric light. A loud explosion was heard when the racing was over and all was quiet. On some of the directors of the grounds proceeding to the spot it was found the safe had been blown open and several hundred pounds been abstracted. The curious part of the business was that no trace of the thieves could be found, and they were never discovered. All sorts of rumours were afloat at the time, and the affair caused quite a sensation.

Foot-racing has almost died out, and mainly through the fault of the runners. Many of these men ran in the interests of bookmakers, and never tried to win although heavily backed. The public were fleeced in the most outrageous manner, and eventually they declined to patronize the running grounds. When sports of this description languish it is generally the fault of the men engaged in them.

Amateur athletic sports are not as well patronized as they ought to be. More interest has, however,

been taken in them of late years, and the inter-
colonial contests have fostered a spirit of rivalry
that has done much to advance the sport. Mainly
through the exertions of Mr. Richard Coombes, the
President of the N. S. W. A. A. A., amateur sports
have become more popular. Mr. Coombes, too, has
been instrumental in promoting harrier clubs, and
he has spent a lot of time and money in the interest
of his pet hobby—amateur athletics.

Bicycling has made rapid strides, and since cash
prizes have come into fashion the competition has
been keen. Mr. Kerr is, or was when I was there,
perhaps the best all-round man in the Colonies. The
Austral Wheel Race in Melbourne is worth a considerable sum to the winner. I am writing entirely
from memory, but I fancy about a couple of hundred
pounds was Mr. Lambton's share when he won. I
saw some splendid races on the Association Ground,
Sydney, in April, 1895, when some hundreds of
pounds were given in cash prizes. Cyclists prefer
the solid cash to a trophy worth about a quarter
its advertised value. Trophies are seldom worth
much.

The *Referee* Football Club members were highly
indignant when having won the Press Football Trophy,
the Secretary of the New South Wales Agricultural
Association, whose society presented the trophy, sent
them a cup that had been used to advertise some

special brand of whiskey. It was returned with thanks, and another cup was afterwards presented, which was accepted. This is the sort of thing generally attaching to trophies. Patent medicine trophies are degrading to any sport, and athletes ought to indignantly decline to be made the medium of advertising.

CHAPTER XVIII.

LIFE ON A SHEEP STATION.

An enormous run. One hundred and thirty thousand sheep shorn. The method of shearing. Some queer characters. A shearers' strike. Dodges resorted to. New hands. How shearers live. Bush shanties. The grog that kills. Take downs. Earnings of shearers.

THERE are some enormous sheep-runs in New South Wales. English farmers may feel inclined to doubt the assertion that a fair-sized farm in the old country would not be considered a large paddock in the Colonies, that is, so far as the acreage is concerned. Yet such is actually the case.

Winbar Station in New South Wales is one of the largest in the Colony. It is the property of the Winbar Pastoral Company, Limited, and is situate on the river Darling, ninety miles below Bourke, the principal town in the Western district. Bourke is about five hundred miles from Sydney.

Winbar is an enormous station, containing an area

14

of 960 square miles, or, in other words, 582,000 acres.
The run extends for a distance of forty-five miles from
end to end, and has a frontage of a hundred miles to
the Darling River. The farthest distance out back is
twenty-nine miles.

The homestead, known as Winbar, is on the river
bank, twenty-three miles from the upper boundary,
and consequently about the centre of the frontage.

The shearing-shed is seventeen miles further down
the river, at the out-station called Campadore, within
five miles of the lower boundary. At this out-station
there is a collection of buildings consisting of over-
seer's cottage, stores, and various huts, also wool-shed
and wool-scouring plant. A brief account of a wool-
shed may not prove uninteresting to your readers.

The wool-shed is a building 130ft. long, built of a
Colonial pine framework on piles two and a-half feet
from the ground, and is closed in with galvanized
corrugated iron. The floor is of gum-boards (two
inches) placed one inch apart. At the southern end
of the shed a space, 40ft. by 45ft., is set apart as a
sweating-pen. This is where the sheep are kept from
exposure to the weather, and prior to being put into
the shearing-pens. At the northern end of the shed
a space, 15ft. by 45ft., is set apart for the wool-tables
and wool-bins, at the former of which five wool sorters
stand and divide the fleeces into various classes of
wool, viz. :—1st and 2nd combing ; 1st, 2nd and 3rd

clothing, pieces, cocks, and bellies. Of course, all these qualities of wool are not found in every fleece : some sheep growing combing-wool and others clothing-wool. The low sorts, such as bellies, pieces, and locks, are found in every fleece.

Between the sweating-pen and wool-sorters' quarters are the shearers. Their portion of the shed is termed the "board," and consists of a space 70ft. long and 8ft. wide, on the eastern and western sides of the building. Fifteen shearers stand on either side of the board, and between them the catching-pens are fixed. These consist of small enclosures about 9ft. square, into which the sheep are put from the sweating-pen. Each pen has a door opening on to the board, and two shearers are supplied with sheep from each pen. There is a passage (called a race) in the centre of the building, the catching-pens being on either side, and a gate opens from each pen into the race ; the race is always kept filled with sheep from the sweating-pen, and as the catching-pens become empty they are filled from this source.

Machines are used to shear the sheep, and it is an interesting sight to see a shed in full work. Most sheds now have machinery, and the old system of hand-shearing has almost died out. Mr. E. Arnold, the manager, informed me that it was nothing more nor less than a stupid prejudice prevented machines from being in use on all stations. Last season (July, 1894) at Winbar 139,000 sheep and lambs were shorn within fourteen weeks, and had it not been for the shearers' strike the work would have been completed in three weeks' less time.

I was in the Colonies during the last shearers' strike, and saw much of the difficulties it caused on the stations. When the roll was called at Winbar, last July, 1894, there were thirty-one police present to preserve law and order. About 120 men were present, none of whom would sign the agreement, and the manager ordered them off the station premises, and they formed a camp, a quarter of a mile below the wool-shed, and selected the public roadway as their camping ground. Eleven men had, however, signed the agreement prior to the roll being called, and with them shearing was commenced.

The Union delegate purchased provisions for the men in the camp, from the hawling steamers on the Darling, and these goods were paid for out of the Union funds. At one time there were 200 men in the camp. They remained there three weeks, during which time pickets were sent out to guard the various approaches to the station. These pickets usually went out in squads of four, all armed with carefully trimmed waddies made from saplings. These waddies were for use should moral suasion not have the desired effect on the non-Union men.

All travellers were stopped and taken to the camp, as many as forty-two being captured in one afternoon. The majority of these men were willing prisoners. The average bushman does not, as a rule, require much pressing to partake of a free meal, especially when he sees the prospect of two or three weeks' board for nothing. All this is at the expense of the Union.

In order to complete the shearing men had to be wired for to Sydney. Winbar was made a "test shed" by the Union on this occasion. Of sixteen men sent from Sydney to Bourke, five deserted in the town. The remainder were sent to the station by special boat. The Unionists were informed by wire from their Bourke agents, and knew when to expect the steamer at Campadore. The Unionists were fully determined to cause a disturbance.

The garrison of police, reduced to fifteen, were on the alert, however, and this, combined with a little manœuvring on the part of the captain of the steamer, prevented a riot. The Unionists expecting the steamer early in the evening had waited round their camp fires until midnight. No boat arriving caused them to conclude it would not come before morning, as cargo-laden steamers are not allowed to travel down stream at night. No doubt the Unionists thought the captain of the steamer would adhere to the rules, for they turned in and evidently slept soundly. The boat came at 5·30 a.m., landed the shearers, and started on her return journey some hours before the Union men were aware anything of the kind had occurred.

The men that came from Sydney were rather a mixed lot. Some of them were at one time well to do, but owing to various causes had suffered reverses of fortune. One was a well-known Sydney trainer, two others had been American cowboys at Wirth's circus. Another was well connected, and his people were well to do, but he had been a bit wild, and had come up under an *alias* to try and knock a cheque together. Another was a nephew of the late Sir Alfred Stephens. One man had been in a prosperous business in New Zealand, but had lost it through dissipation. His wife, the daughter of a departed knight, is in receipt of £300 a year, and is living apart from her husband.

Most of these men had never shorn a sheep, probably had never seen one shorn, but they were all anxious and willing to learn, and in most cases succeeded. A few got tired of trying to shear, and were given employment as shed hands at weekly wages, and they were really hard-working fellows. The shearers have a hut built of pine slabs with iron roof to themselves, and the shed hands (rouseabouts) have a similar building. The wool scourers also live separately. In all, there are about a hundred men employed at the shed during the shearing, and amongst them are some queer characters. One man was named "Silent Billy," and it was a nickname well merited, as he did not speak on an average more than twice a day. The shearer's mode of dress is both simple and inexpensive, merely a pair of moleskin pants and a merino singlet or flannel. He seldom wears socks or an overshirt. In many instances, the shearer works barefooted, or he has on shoes made out of a piece of bagging or woolpack with string for laces. On Sunday, the luxury of a pair of boots, and, perhaps, socks, is indulged in, and if the shearer is extravagant, he may put on a clean shirt and pair of moles. A coat is sometimes noticed, and, perhaps, a necktie on rare occasions.

The daily routine is seldom varied. Work commences at 6 a.m. and lasts until 8 a.m., when an hour is allowed for breakfast. From 9 to 10.20, and then twenty minutes for a smoke, after which shearing goes on until noon. At 1 p.m. they resume until 2.20, when there is another twenty minutes for a smoke. They then shear until 4 p.m., and then have twenty minutes for tea; this over, they go on until 5.30. Then if the weather is warm enough some go for a swim in the river. At 6 p.m. supper is served. Then yarning commences, and at the tale-spinning process shearers are good hands. Perhaps the monotony is broken by someone informing the company the Unionists are unusually active, and some have been seen in the vicinity of the premises. Immediately the doors and windows are looked to and the barricades got ready in case of the worst happening. One or two revolvers are inspected. The excitement spreads, and by the time the report has reached the far end of the hut it has been added to, and the last man informed is told that a large body of armed Unionists are outside thirsting for his blood. Lights are out at 9.30 p.m., when the bulk of the men turn in.

Sunday is devoted to rabbit hunting, bird-nesting, and fishing, with an occasional game at cricket; the shearers, however, are very poor cricketers.

A public-house is situated within one mile of the shed. It is kept by an elderly widow, who has buried three husbands, a fact which indicates the quality of the grog kept on the premises. The home-made grog business is a common practice amongst bush publicans, owing to there being no proper police supervision. Some queer things occur at these bush shanties, and in many of them it is not safe for anyone with money to go into an hotel (?), for if the publican cannot rob the man himself he puts someone on to do it for him.

The following is a fact: One man who had earned nearly £1,000 within a few months at rabbiting went to an hotel and called for three drinks—one for himself, another for a hanger-on of the publican, and a third for the publican. He then produced a cheque for £970, and told the publican to "take it out of that." Of course there was no change on the premises, and the cheque had to be sent to the bank and the change obtained by first mail. Whether this was done I cannot say, but I know the rabbiter stayed eighteen days at the hotel and went away penniless, having transferred his right, title, and interest to the publican. About £100 would have bought all the grog in the house. This is only one of many instances in which men are robbed by unprincipled ruffians, who ought never to have been allowed to keep an hotel.

Life on a station at shearing time is not all pleasure, especially in these days when most stations work short handed. The low price of wool makes it necessary to keep expenses down. The musterers who keep the shed going with sheep are the hardest worked men on the station. They are kept busy day after day from early morning until sunset, and sometimes even later. Sundays and week days are all alike, nothing but sheep work. It is surprising the amount of work station horses will do when fed upon grass alone.

Occasionally some big tallies are made during shearing. One man's record for one week was 1,191, and his total for eleven weeks was 7,292. For this

he got £72 18s. 5d. Against this was his tucker
bill, £8 12s. 10d., his comb and cutters cost him
£1 10s. 6d., so that he netted £62 15s. 1d. His
highest daily total was 212.

Shearers that can shear from 100 to 120 sheep
per day are considered the best men to employ. The
big tally men set a bad example to the others,
and cause "running," which means bad shearing.
The 200 a-day men are not, as a rule, first class
shearers. No man can shear that number within
eight hours properly.

CHAPTER XIX.

Theatrical management. Class of performances. A trip with
  George Rignold.   Her Majesty's Theatre.   A curious
  "Martha."   Brough and Boucicault.   Williamson and
  Musgrove. Their productions. A yarn. "Widow O'Brien."
  John F. Sheridan.   Some comedians.   Elton's armour.
  Visitors to the Colonies. An excellent school. Apprecia-
  tive audiences. A variety of notes.

MANY celebrated actors and actresses have visited
Australia, and it is significant that most of them have
been eager to pay a return trip. Colonials are good
judges of plays and acting, assertions to the contrary
notwithstanding.   A second-rate performance finds no
favour with them, and it would be useless for any actor
or actress, who could not succeed in England or elsewhere, paying a visit to Australia in order to meet
with a more favourable reception.

So well have various Australian managers catered
for the public that nothing but *the best* will satisfy
them. The prices charged for admission to the theatres

are exceedingly moderate when the high-class nature of the performances is considered. It is only upon very rare occasions the ordinary prices are raised. The highest ruling price is five shillings in the dress circle or reserved stalls, three shillings in the ordinary stalls, two shillings in the upper circle, and a shilling, sometimes sixpence, in the gallery. If theatrical managers can make these prices pay, there must be a considerable margin of profit where double the charge is made for admission. Rents and taxes may not be so high as in the old country, but travelling expenses are very heavy, and long distances separate the principal towns. Plays are mounted lavishly, and both in opera, comedy, and drama the dresses and scenery will compare more than favourably with the average London theatre. Such firms as Messrs. Williamson and Musgrove, and Messrs. Brough and Boucicault must spend enormous sums of money in the course of a year in theatrical properties. Mr. George Rignold and Mr. Bland Holt, in the sensational drama, mount their plays on a costly scale, and the scenic artists are clever men. Such scene painters as Messrs. Gordon, Phil. Goachter, John Brunton, Spong and Clint, would be hard to beat for really artistic productions.

As for the theatres, the Lyceum and Her Majesty's at Sydney, and the Princesses in Melbourne, are not surpassed by more than three or four London houses, and are ahead of many of the provincial theatres in England.

I am not painting the attractions of the Colonies in too glowing colours, and I feel convinced actors and actresses who have visited Australia, and been a success there, will bear out my remarks.

The trip I undertook to Sydney in the " Liguria " in 1884 was to me a memorable one.   On board I found Mr. George Rignold and his amiable wife ; Miss Kate Bishop, a popular London favourite, who played in that enormously successful run of " Our Boys " at the Vaudeville ; Mr. Brian Darley, and a gentleman not at that time connected with the profession, Mr. L. J. Lohr, now the husband of "Miss Kate Bishop," a lady whose acquaintance he made on the ·teamer. To balance the theatrical element, we had on board Archbishop, now Cardinal, Moran and his clerical staff. Although the exact opposite of each other in every respect, Cardinal Moran and Mr. George Rignold got on very well together, and argued in an amicable manner. We had several lively characters on board, and a mock Parliament was formed, in which Mr. Rignold figured as the member for Hades, the heat of the Red Sea, where he was elected to the constituency, no doubt favouring that locality. The member for Mount Sinai was suggested by an alleged glimpse of that mountain in the distance. We had some furious debates at night, and, owing to the amount of obstruction, at times attempts were made to gag the members. When Henry V. occupied the chair his massive proportions commanded respect, and "handsome George" ruled the members with a rod of iron.

Mr. Lohr, now a prominent theatrical agent, and manager of the Criterion Theatre, Sydney, was called the umpire. Disputes were often referred to him, and he generally ended them by making the disputants "shout" for the other members of the house. The purveyor of liquid refreshments rejoiced in the name of King. He generally took a nap in a hammock strung up near the bar, when the weather was hot. When calmly sleeping he was sometimes surprised, on being roused, to find one end of his hammock let down, and that he was standing straight up. Explanation naturally followed, but as a matter of course, the culprit who let him down was never discovered.

Mr. George Rignold went into partnership in Australia with Mr. James Allison, since dead, but when he took over Her Majesty's Theatre as sole lessee, it was a lucky stroke of business for him. He has made money there, and, although Mr. Rignold is constantly lamenting the bad times, I would not mind having the balance at his bank. An excellent stock company was got together at Her Majesty's, and several of the members have been with Mr. Rignold ever since he took over the theatre. As a stage-manager Mr. Rignold excels, and such dramas as "The Lights of London," "Silver King," "Romany Rye," "In the Ranks," "My Partner," and many others, were splendidly staged. His Shakesperian productions were also excellent, more especially "Henry V.," "A Midsummer Night's Dream," "Julius Cæsar," "Merry Wives of Windsor," and others. He also gave a very fine production of "Faust," which Mr. Gilbert Parker had a hand in arranging for him. A curious scene occurred in a production of "Faust," by Mr. Rignold at Brisbane, in the Old Theatre Royal. Mrs. George Rignold was not well enough to play Martha, and when I saw Mr. J. W. Sweeney walk on in that character, I thought the shock would have been too much to bear. Mr. Sweeney is a big, jolly, rollicking Irishman, and how he got into Martha's garments is one of those mysteries he alone can unravel. He confided to me afterwards, he was so terribly compressed, and had such a horror of hearing Martha's apparel straining and cracking that he became utterly oblivious of the Mephistophelian whispers of Mr. George Rignold. Mr. Sweeney struggled desperately with Martha, and it says much for his ability that very few people in the audience recognized in Marguerite's nurse the big burly Irishman that so often delighted them as a policeman or as a sailor of the most rollicking type.

For seven or eight years Mr. Rignold kept Her

Majesty's open with very few breaks. He has done an enormous amount of work, and played in scores of dramas and plays. Prominent amongst the members of his company was Miss Kate Bishop (Mrs. Lohr). Mr. Jewitt, a clever actor, took Mr. Brian Darley's place, and he in turn has gone to America, where he has been successful. Children's pantomime at Christmas is a feature of Mr. Rignold's productions, and he generally has a successful run with it. Mr. J. P. Macdonald, his acting manager, was in front of the house for many years. I was sorry to hear of his death in St. Vincent's Hospital, Sydney, since my return to England. Mr. Rignold was very much attached to him, and was present with him to the last. Mr. and Mrs. Rignold are returning to London, and the well-known manager has at length decided to give up Her Majesty's Theatre. He will, I am certain, have a splendid benefit before he leaves Sydney, and no actor will better have deserved it.

In Mr. Rignold's dressing-room I have had many a pleasant chat, when he was making-up for some heroic part in which he had to go through unheard of dangers and trials before the curtain fell on the final scene. It is terribly hot work sometimes with the thermometer at a hundred or so in the shade. When Madame Sarah Bernhardt visited Sydney, she appeared at Her Majesty's, and used Mr. Rignold's room to dress in. The great actress was received with unbounded enthusiasm in Australia, and was much gratified at her reception. I had an interview with Mr. Abbey before her arrival, and he acknowledged it was a risky speculation to pilot Madame Bernhardt in Australia, but added, he thought the result would be financially satisfactory, and so I believe it was.

On the occasion of Madame Bernhardt's appearances, the prices were raised to ten shillings in the dress circle, which was always full, as in fact were all parts of this large theatre. I think her La Tosca was the favourite character, but Cleopatra and Camile ran it close. Her reception on her arrival in Sydney was a typical Australian welcome, hearty and freely given.

Messrs. Williamson and Musgrove have always catered well for the theatrical public, and at the Lyceum in Sydney and the Princess's in Melbourne some of the best performances in Australia have been given. "The Firm," as they are called, formerly had the old Theatre Royal in Sydney, but when a fire took place there they had to go elsewhere, and the Lyceum, then in course of erection, was taken. It is a large handsome theatre, with a fine stage, and beautifully upholstered. I have seen some fine performances here. The Gaiety Company, the Royal Comic Opera Company, the Italian Opera Company, Edward Terry and Company, appeared here.

In the first Gaiety Company Miss Nellie Farren and the late Fred Leslie appeared, and the reception they met with was one to be remembered. Mr. Lonnen was not so popular as Fred Leslie, but he scored a distinct success.

Messrs. Brough and Boucicault have done much to popularise high-class comedies and farcical comedies in Australia, and their Shakesperian productions have cost a pile of money. It would be difficult to find a better company than that of Messrs. Brough and Boucicault. Both these gentlemen, as their names indicate, come of a good old stock of actors, and they are worthy representatives of the names they bear. Mr. Pinero's plays are especially suitable to the company, and Mrs. Brough, as Paula in " The Second Mrs. Tanqueray," gave a magnificent performance. The play was well received, but curiosity had much to do with attracting the large audiences. Mr. Titherage is the leading member of the Brough and Boucicault Company, and he is an admirable actor, much after the style of Mr. Hare. Mr. Ward is another brilliant member of an all-round brilliant set. Mrs. Brough, Miss Brenda Gibson, Miss Noble, Miss Pattie Brown, Miss Romer, Mr. George Carey, and Mr. Brough and Mr. Boucicault are all great favourites with the public. The plays produced by this company are always mounted in the most lavish manner. No expense is spared and every detail is complete.

It would be impossible here to enumerate one-half the plays I have seen produced in the Colonies. There has, however, been a uniform excellence noticeable throughout.

Mrs. Robert Brough compares favourably with the best actresses we have had in Australia. She is a refined graceful actress, has a melodious voice, and an admirable stage presence. The rapidity with which she has come to the front is remarkable. She has undertaken an enormous amount of work, and it can be said of her, with perfect fairness, she is equally good in light comedy as in more serious plays of the Tanqueray type. She plays Lady Betty Noel in the "Amazons" as well as Beatrice in "Much Ado About Nothing." Her Beatrice is a very fine performance, and this and Paula in "The Second Mrs. Tanqueray" are certainly two of her best characters. As Niobe in the screaming farcical comedy of that name, she is also at her best. There is no more popular actress on the Australian stage than Mrs. Robert Brough.

Mr. George Carey tells a story about the Brough and Boucicault Company in New Zealand. They were playing in Auckland. Mr. Carey went into a well-known tobacconist's for some of the fragrant weed.

"Ever go to the theatre?" asks Carey.

"Not often; but I'm going this week," said the cigar merchant.

"Oh!" said Carey, "What night?"

" Friday."

" Let me see, what's on ? " said Carey.

" A play that has been much talked about," said the man in a whisper. " It's a bit of an eye opener, they tell me."

" Dear me," said Carey, wondering which piece in their extensive repertoire could be termed an eye opener.

" What is the name of the piece ? " asked Carey.

" The Second Mrs. Langtry," said the shopkeeper.

Carey, stifling his laughter, said he hoped he would enjoy it. When George Carey ran a company of his own he visited Brisbane. In that company was Mr. Albert Norman, then a young inexperienced actor, now one of the leading villains on the stage. When I last saw him he was playing with Mr. Bland Holt's Company at the Royal, Sydney, in " The Fatal Card." Carey played " The Three Hats " in Brisbane, and also " Pink Dominoes," both being successful.

I was staying at the Queen's Hotel at the time, and a friend of mine was seriously ill there. As he was getting melancholy I fancied a good rousing laugh would do him good, so I brought George Carey down to dinner.

I took him to my friend's room, seated him on the bed, and said,

" Tell him some yarns, there's a good fellow."

George Carey started, and if I had not put the

stopper on him at the end of half-an-hour, I verily believe my friend would have died from exhaustion caused by over much laughter. Carey's medicine did him no end of good.

Mr. Frank Thornton stayed at the Queen's when playing "The Private Secretary" at the Royal. One night we were roused from sweet repose by hearing noises in Mr. Thornton's room.

I rushed out, and opening his door saw the Rev. Robert Spalding doing a rat hunt round the bed-room with an umbrella in one hand and a candle in the other. He was in, not his surplice, but a garment resembling it in colour.

He implored me not to spoil sport, so I left him to it.

Mr. Thornton was very amusing off the stage as well as on. I was at the Royal, in a side box, one night with a friend. During the course of the play, "The Private Secretary," Mr. Cattermole sits heavily down on the lid of a box in which the Rev. Spalding takes refuge. Mr. Harwood played Cattermole, and he nearly squeezed Frank Thornton to death when he got into the box.

Thornton, when he took refuge under a table, spied us in the box. He could not be seen by the audience. The grimaces he made and the manner in which he expressed how he had been jammed in the box, made us roar with laughter.

Mr. John F. Sheridan, "Widow O'Brien," was and still is a friend of mine. I have met him in the West of New South Wales, and as near to London as Sandown Park. When I was editing the *Daily Times* in Bathurst, Mr. Sheridan came along with his company. They opened at the School of Arts, in Dorothy. Next morning in came Sheridan to my office followed by his big black retriever dog.

"Going to give us a notice?" says Sheridan.

"If I've got time," I replied. "Better write one yourself, John. At any rate, draw out the plot."

I may mention that every editor of a country newspaper likes to get a helping hand when he can.

Sheridan sat down and tied his dog to the leg of the chair he sat upon.

"The Widder" seized copy paper, flourished a pen, and dived into the plot of "Dorothy."

He had been writing for about a quarter of an hour when no less a personage than the Bishop of Bathurst, Dr. Camidge, a learned, clever man, and as popular a citizen as ever resided there, walked in. He had a fox terrier at his heels.

I entered into conversation with his lordship, and his lordship's dog entered into conversation with Sheridan's dog.

The Bishop opened the door, bade us good morning, and Sheridan politely rose.

As he got up from his chair the retriever thought it a favourable opportunity to follow the Bishop's dog, and he bolted, dragging the chair away and letting "The Widder" down on the floor.

Up jumped Sheridan and bolted after his dog.

I went to the door and saw a race going on between the dogs and their masters.

Presently in came Sheridan with the retriever in tow.

"That's the first race I ever had with a Bishop," said Sheridan; "I beat him on the post."

If ever I wanted to find his lordship in the city I invariably looked for his terrier.

The dog generally seated itself outside the house or public building the Bishop went into. It was a sure sign he was inside.

I once remarked to his lordship that it would never do for a journalist to own a dog like that, as the faithful animal would give him away by sitting calmly outside houses of entertainment.

Mr. John F. Sheridan made a great hit with "Fun on the Bristol," and he was always alluded to as "The Widder."

His agent, when first I knew him, was Mr. Samuels.

Samuels tells the yarn himself, so there can be no harm in repeating it.

There was a heavy amount for stamps down in the bill he presented to Sheridan.

"I say, Samuels, what had you for dinner?" said Sheridan.

Samuels thought a moment and mentioned one or two items he had fancied on the bill of fare.

"And had you a good breakfast?" asked Sheridan.

"Yes," says Samuels, who could not make out what "The Widder" was driving at.

"You're quite sure you're not ill?" said Sheridan, with an anxious look on his face.

"Never was better," said Samuels; "what makes you ask?"

"I fancied you might have been living on postage stamps," said Sheridan, "judging by the amount in the bill."

It was an amusing sight to see Mr. Sheridan making up for Widow O'Brien. Where he stuck all the pins was to me a mystery. The way he put up his back hair was most ludicrous. A more perfect make up there could not be. All the time Mr. Sheridan was engaged in turning himself into a fascinating widow he chatted to me in his dressing-room, and told stories of the time when he was merely a clever dancer and had not developed into a full-blown actor.

Theatrical companies have some curious experiences when travelling up country in Australia. In the more remote parts they have to go by coach, and when heavy rain has been falling they occasionally get stuck up in a bog or have their luggage washed away when fording a river. At Bourke not so very long ago a theatrical company had the misfortune to see the roof blown off the theatre.

One company struck hard times and bad luck, and when the night for the performance in a country town came the hall-keeper went on the stage and demanded his salary.

The manager intimated it would be paid after the play was over, but this did not satisfy the man.

"Very well," he said, "no pay no gas," and he declined to turn on the lights.

The Royal Comic Opera Company, organized by Messrs. Williamson and Musgrove, has been touring the Colonies for some years, and all the latest operatic successes have been produced by them. Miss Nellie Stewart is a great favourite and never fails to secure a hearty reception. Mr. Charles Ryley, Mr. Wallace Brownlow, Mr. William Elton, Mr. Charles Lauri, Mr. Howard Vernon, Mr. Tapley, and many other good actors and actresses have been connected with this company. Mr. Williamson is very popular, and he is very fond of all kinds of sport, racing especially. Most actors in the Colonies appear to be fond of racing, Mr. Brough amongst the number.

Mr. and Mrs. Lohr (Miss Bishop) resided next to me at Sydney at one time. During their absence they let the house to Mr. William Elton and his family. He was engaged at that time with the Royal Comic Opera Company. One morning the famous comedian sent to my house to borrow a hammer, and shortly after I heard a terrific row at the back of the house. On looking out of the window I saw Mr. Elton working vigorously in battering a kerosine tin, which gradually assumed the shape of armour. I fancy he was making a suit of shining armour either for the Duke of Plasa Toro in the "Gondoliers" or for his famous character in the "Old Guard." Mr. Elton is an immense favourite. When he left the company Mr. Charles Lauri took his place and speedily became popular.

Mr. Tapley married Miss Violet Varley, a member of the company, and I was sorry to hear of this clever little lady's death in Melbourne. Miss Varley had a bright future before her, and her premature end will be much regretted. This opera company has received several recruits from Pollard's Juvenile Opera Troupe, a clever combination of youngsters. Miss Varley and Miss Flora Graupner, were both members of the Pollard's, and Miss May Pollard was in the Royal Comic Opera Company when I left.

I once attended a rehearsal on the stage of the Princess's Theatre, Melbourne, of the Pollard juveniles, when Mr. Fred Duval was the manager. It was amusing to see the youngsters at work. They were all as full of mischief as a set of schoolboys and schoolgirls, and Mr. Pollard must have been blessed with no end of patience. These clever juveniles have produced as many as four different operas in a week.

When Mr. J. L. Toole visited the Colonies he met with a hearty reception. Socially, he was a success, but, from what I saw of him at Sydney, he did not catch on with the public. Mr. Toole's style is peculiarly his own, and his humour did not appear to strike the Colonial audiences. This may sound like heresy in such a celebrated actor's case, but it is nevertheless a fact. I do not think Mr. Toole was at his best.

Many a time I have laughed at his wonderful acting in my juvenile days, and I shall never forget the first time I saw Toole in the pigskin.

Mrs. Bernard Beere was a decided success. Her style exactly hit Australian audiences. Mr. Charles Warner met with a fair share of success, and appeared in some of his best plays. "Drink" was as popular as any of them.

Mrs. Brown Potter and Mr. Kyrle Bellew were also well received. They produced a remarkable play "Hero and Leander," which afforded Mrs. Potter an opportunity of appearing in a *very* cool costume in hot weather, and Mr. Bellew when "Cast up by the Sea," was in flesh-coloured tights and very little even of these. The effect was extraordinary, when he rolled on to the stage out of the sad sea waves, and Mrs. Brown Potter went into hysterics over his scantily clothed body. There was also a desperate scene when Hero came into Leander's chamber dripping with water from the Hellespont, and the curtain was discreetly lowered before matters came to a climax. Mr. T. V. Twinning was their manager, and a real good fellow he is. He is now lessee of the Corinthian Theatre, Calcutta, and I recently met him in London, when we had a chat about old times in the Colonies.

Miss Genevieve Ward and Mr. W. H. Vernon, were decidedly successful, and in " Forget-me-Not," and " Mammon," and " Jane Shore," they had every opportunity of showing their great abilities. Mr. Wybert Reeve as Count Fosco in the " Woman in White," was a real treat, and he has successfully managed the Adelaide Theatre for some years ?

Madame Melba will have a far different reception when she returns to Australia to that she received at Bathurst some years ago when such a scanty audience assembled to hear her that the concert was abandoned. And yet the Bathurstians rather pride themselves upon their knowledge of good singing and music.

I ought not to omit Mr. Goodman, the well-known

manager for Messrs. Williamson and Musgrove at the Lyceum, Sydney. "Goody" is a popular man, and when his duties permit of his taking a holiday he generally goes on a fishing expedition, returning laden with spoil. He fills his basket as well as he fills "the house."

Miss Olga Nethersole was one of the most successful actresses I saw in the Colonies. She was supported by an excellent company including Mr. Charles Cartwright, and her tour was profitable. Miss Janet Achurch introduced Ibsen to Colonial audiences, but his plays were not much thought of. Mr. Lionel Rignold was not such a success as Mr. William Rignold. When the "Merry Wives of Windsor" was produced at Her Majesty's, Mr. William Rignold's Falstaff was considered a masterly performance. He also played in several dramas, in all of which he was successful. Mr. Walter Bentley was at first well received, but his popularity waned, and Mr. Milne found Shakespeare a frost.

Some years ago Mr. W. J. Holloway was remarkably fortunate in his Shakesperian productions, and also in a round of modern dramas. Miss Essie Jenyns was the great attraction, and the stage lost an admirable actress when she married Mr. Wood, the wealthy collier proprietor of Newcastle. The Majeronis gave some fine performances. Miss Myra Kemble is another Colonial favourite. Several good variety companies visited Australia, and the Cragg family astonished every one with their clever acrobatic feats. Miss Billie Barlow, Fred Mason, Frank Lincoln were all well pleased with the reception they met with. Enough has been written to show Australians patronise the theatres well, and a good company can always rely upon a hearty reception. It does not always follow that a London success will prove a Colonial success, and unsuitable plays are often brought out by men who ought to have better judgment. In high class comedy no one is more appreciated than Pinero whose plays are sure to prove a draw. The Adelphi drama and Mr. Geo. Sims' plays are sure to be profitable productions. Mr. Haddon Chambers' play, "The Idler," was first produced in Australia by Miss Olga Nethersole, and it was at once a success, more so than the same author's "Captain Swift." Mr. George Darrell is another Australian author-actor who has produced many local plays with varying success. Mr. George Leitch first produced his dramatised version of Marcus Clark's "His Natural Life," at the Theatre Royal, Brisbane. I was present at the opening performance which dragged on until the small hours of the morning. The *Brisbane Courier* gave it a notice of several columns, which I fancy must have been written up at intervals during the preceding week.

There is plenty of theatrical talent in the Colonies,

and a good local man always receives a fair chance of success. Mr. Harry Rickards since he took over the Garrick Theatre and turned it into the Tivoli, has made a fortune. He has succeeded in running a cheap price house, the highest charge for admission to a good show being two shillings. Since the depression set in things theatrical have not been good, and many actors have been out of harness. Various means of raising money have been devised. The theatrical fêtes in Sydney and Melbourne were big successes, and were held on the largest grounds available. Benefits are numerous, and when an actor runs short of cash he can generally induce his comrades to give him a benefit in a theatre "kindly lent for the occasion" by an obliging manager.

Taken throughout, the life of an actor in the Colonies is enjoyable, although he has an immense amount of study and hard work to get through. The constant changes in the bill cause frequent rehearsals, and there are no long runs as in London theatres. The Colonial stage is an excellent school to acquire experience in, for the actor has to play many parts in the course of a year. As a stepping-stone to higher things in the profession a tour of the Colonies has few equals.

CHAPTER XX.

Winding up. Colonial life. Agitators. "Going home." End
of the gallop.

In the preceding chapters I have endeavoured to give
a brief account of how I passed over ten pleasant years
in Australia. I trust the many shortcomings this book
contains will be overlooked in the same kind and
friendly manner as they have been in other works I
have written. It has been my endeavour to write of
men and things as I found them, and from an ordinary
everyday view.

For the Colonies as a home I can only write in
terms of the highest praise. The life would not suit
every one, but for a man who desires to live pretty
much as he likes, and not be bound down by conven-
tional forms, it is a thoroughly enjoyable existence.

Once the taste for Colonial life has been acquired,
it grows and expands until it becomes part of a man's
nature.

Few people who have resided abroad for many years care to settle down permanently in the old country again. If a married man, with a young family and a moderate capital, asked my advice, I should strongly urge him to make Australia his home.

There is more chance there for such a man. Although competition is keen, there is always room for good men.

Remittance men are the bane of the Colonies. They are no good to themselves or anyone else. They invariably run down everything Colonial, and brag about their connections, who have sent them out in order to get rid of them. It always seems to me the height of ingratitude for a man to run down a country in which he is making a living merely because it is not the land of his birth, and there are hundreds of Britishers who do this.

England would be badly off without her Colonies, and the Colonies would not get on so well without aid from the mother country.

In years to come Australia will, no doubt, be a second United States, but there will not be the same anti-English feeling that is unfortunately at times noticeable in America.

Colonials almost invariably speak of England as "home." "Are you going home?" is the question asked when a trip to the old country is contemplated.

With the increased facilities for travelling afforded

16

by the great steamship companies, a trip to England
is now regarded as quite an ordinary holiday. The
friendly feeling between the two countries is thus
cemented. The visits of Australian cricketers, scullers,
and athletes to England certainly strengthen these
ties, as also do the visits of an English Eleven, or
prominent actors and actresses, to Australia.

A bond of fellowship appears to exist between
sportsmen all over the world, and no one could have
met with a more friendly reception than I have
experienced from the sportsmen I have met since my
return to England. I hope I may have an opportunity to return their kindness on the other side of the
globe.

Home life in the Colonies is most enjoyable, and I
have never regretted the time it became necessary for
me to make a home of my own and to forsake the
roving life of a bachelor.

In answer to the question " Is marriage a failure,"
I give a decided " No." The unfortunate Colonial
bachelor has not commenced to know how to live. It is
pure selfishness keeps the bulk of the men single, and
a selfish man is a blot upon creation. Sporting men,
as a rule, are not selfish, at least such has been my experience. In the words of a once popular song, they

> " Do not think you're poorer for helping a friend
> With a pound or two when he's in need,
> And you're certainly worse if you worship your purse,
> And give way to miserly greed."

To young active men, possessed of pluck and average brain power, and with an aptitude for work, I say, " Make your home in the Colonies, by all means."

When there are thousands more homes in Australia she will be the richer. Work comes with population. It is lack of population creates an "unemployed." Every man added to a community makes work for some other man.

Australia, like other countries, suffers from un-principled agitators who fatten upon the working men they befool with their sophistry. The real Labour party in the Colonies are the men who build up the country's future by work, not the men who mouth and rave and draw their means of subsistence from the workmen's funds.

We do not pay doctors to give bad advice, why should these labour agitators, whose remedies are worse than the diseases they propose to cure, be feed heavily ?

It is not the sporting proclivities of the Australians that is their ruination, it is the idle worthless ranters miscalled labour leaders. I am not alluding to the Labour Members. As a whole they are a sensible body of men and do good for their cause in a legitimate way.

In this book of fragments nothing has been over-drawn. I have jotted down, from memory alone, nearly the whole of the contents. If there are slight errors they are from lapse of memory not from any intention to misrepresent. It is customary for some writers of books to call publishers nasty names. I have never found occasion for this. I sometimes think the boot might rightly be placed on the other leg and publishers could, no doubt, say unutterable things of authors. In sporting parlance I never care how much a publisher makes out of me provided I get my "whack," which, so far, I consider I have done.

I started with a preliminary canter and have finished my course. I hope the staying powers of my readers have not been too sorely tried. I can only hope they have enjoyed my yarn as much as I did those ten years "On and Off the Turf in Australia."

THE END.

SIMMONS & BOTTEN, Limited, Printers, Shoe Lane, London, E.C.

GEORGE ROUTLEDGE & SONS'
LIST OF ANNOUNCEMENTS.

My Travels in Europe and America, 1893. By His Highness the RAJA-I-RAJGAN JAJAT JIT SINGH of Kapurthala (The Rajah). With Photogravure Portraits. Limited to 300 copies, price 21*s.*

W. H. Prescott's Works. A New Édition de luxe, in twelve volumes, New Type and Portraits (limited to 50 Copies for the English Market), price £8.

The Complete Cambridge Edition of Longfellow's Poems, with a new Biography, Chronological Order of the Poems, full Index, etc. 3*s.* 6*d.* The only Complete Edition that can be issued in this Country.

The Magnificent Edition of The Three Musketeers, with the original Illustrations by MAURICE LELOIR, which was issued last year in two volumes, Paper Covers, price 42*s.*, is beautifully bound in cloth, gilt edges, at the same price.

Price £16 12s.

The Hundred Books of Sir John Lubbock are now completed in One Hundred Volumes. Special terms are offered to those who purchase a set, forming the most complete Library in the World. *A List of the Series, arranged according to prices and subjects, will be sent on application.*

Price 7s. 6d. each.

1. **The New Every Boy's Book.** An entirely new book of Sports, arranged on a novel plan. Reset in New Type, with original Illustrations and Diagrams. Edited by W. A. BLEW of *The Field.* 18th Edition.

2. **Discoveries and Inventions of The Nineteenth Century.** Edited by ROBERT ROUTLEDGE. A New Edition brought up to the present period. 11th Edition.

New 5s. Juvenile Books.

IN LARGE CROWN 8vo, FULL OF ILLUSTRATIONS.

1. **Every Boy's Stories.** With 32 Full-page Plates.
2. **Every Girl's Stories.** With 24 Full-page Plates.
3. **Every Child's Stories.** With 32 Full-page Plates.

Written by the best Authors, and destined to become the three leading books of Juvenile Literature.

ROUTLEDGE'S NEW SERIES OF 3s. 6d. COPYRIGHT NOVELS.

1. **Two Women and a Fool.** By H. CHATFIELD-TAYLOR.
2. **A Sawdust Doll.** By Mrs. REGINALD DE KOVEN.
3. **Poppæa.** By JULIEN GORDON.
4. **A Son of Æsau.** By MINNIE GILMORE.
5. **The Woman Who Stood Between.** By MINNIE GILMORE.
6. **One Woman's Wisdom.** By A. MURPHY.

Price 3s. 6d.

British Moths. By J. W. TUTT. With numerous Woodcuts and 12 Plates of Figures in Colours.

Two New Juvenile Books by the Popular Writer for Boys, the Rev. H. C. ADAMS, M.A. Price 3s. 6d. each.

1. **Fighting His Way.** With Full-page Illustrations by A. W. COOPER.
2. **School and University.** With Full-page Illustrations by A. W. COOPER.

A NEW AND BEAUTIFUL EDITION OF ALEXANDRE DUMAS' NOVELS, printed from New Plates, to be known as the D'ARTAGNAN EDITION. Issued in Monthly Volumes.

Price 3s. 6d. each.

The **Three Musketeers.** Two Volumes. Now Ready.

A NEW EDITION OF VICTOR HUGO'S NOVELS, To be known as the NOTRE DAME EDITION. Price 3s. 6d. each volume.

Notre Dame. Two Volumes. Now Ready.

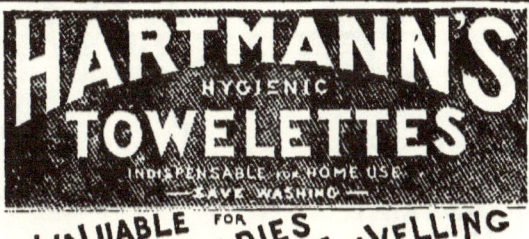

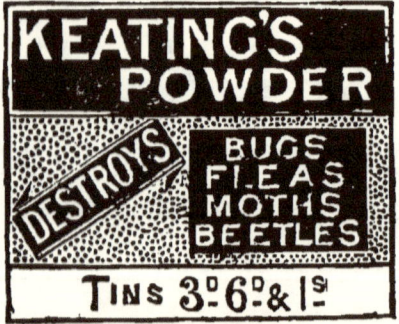

www.ingramcontent.com/pod-product-compliance
Lightning Source LLC
Chambersburg PA
CBHW030758020726
47499CB00006B/1675